My Heart to Find

ELIN ANNALISE

My Heart To Find

First edition published in November 2020
This edition published in May 2021 by Ineja Press

Cover Design by Elin Annalise and Sarah Anderson
Interior Formatting by Sarah Anderson

Paperback ISBN: 978-1-912369-30-0
eBook ISBN: 978-1-912369-29-4

The author can be contacted via email at ElinAnnalise@outlook.com

Second edition, May 2021

ELIN ANNALISE

My Heart to Find

INEJA PRESS

ONE

Cara

IF THERE'S ONE place I never want to be again, it's in this club with the too-loud music and the too-hot artificial glares.

My head pounds, and my vision blurs. A grating sensation—the usual one—fills my head. It feels like a miniscule drill is digging into my skull. I wince as the pain comes. Three flashes of it. The pain is like a volcano, hot and bubbling and consuming, leaving me panting and breathless. Dark spots hover in front of my eyes for a moment. My chest shudders, but it shudders out of sync with the rest of my body, creating a jarring sensation.

I grunt. Well they can't say I'm *boring* now. And I try to focus on that—my triumph at proving River and everyone else who wrote mean stuff about me online wrong. Because *boring people* don't go to clubs. *Boring people* don't try to dance under bright lights—even if I didn't quite manage it because I couldn't go too near other people. But *boring people* are tucked up in bed at this ungodly hour, not dancing the night away.

Not that I'm dancing. My body's too broken for that.

Not that I'm boring either—I'm chronically ill. There's a world of difference. I shouldn't have let the nasty comments get to me. Jana told me not to. She said I've got nothing to prove by coming out here.

But she doesn't get it. She doesn't live a life where she's referred to as *the sick girl* or *the psycho* or *the boring, ill one* or the *faker.* And maybe forcing myself to come out to this club with Jana was a bad idea because it could fuel the 'faker' rumors, making it seem that I'm actually well enough to be here.

And I'm not.

I'm *so* not.

"Do you want to go outside?"

I look up. A man's staring at me from a few feet away—concerned? I mean, no wonder; I have sweat pouring off me. His face is also shiny with perspiration, albeit not as much as I can feel on mine . The flashing lights make his skin look an eerie green, but they also emphasize the strong, heavy features of his face. A slightly hooked nose. Thick eyebrows. He'd be great to draw a caricature of. Could easily be a villain in my cartoon strip.

I breathe deeply. Yes. I need fresh air.

I need to get out of here.

"Definitely," I shout back, but I can't even hear my own voice over the pounding music.

I look around. I lost sight of Jana at least half an hour ago. Well, she's probably outside too. Clubs aren't really her scene. We're only here because it's her cousin's birthday. And Anastacia is one of those people that you don't say no to.

The man reaches for my hand—

No!

I flinch as he makes contact. I pull my hand back quickly, and my breathing quickens. He gives me an odd look, then gestures for me to walk ahead of him in the direction of an exit.

I do, the whole time trying to still my racing mind. My fingers feel burnt where he touched them. I want to wipe them on something. Hell, even wash them. But the bathroom here is full of vomiting teenagers, and I can't go in there, no matter how strong the urge to wash my hands—or to empty my bladder—gets. And I can't wipe my hands on my dress. I just can't. Getting outside—into the fresh air—sounds good, even though most of the time I'm scared of the outdoors, of all the dangers it holds. But being outdoors is now preferable to being stuck in here, with sweat particles in the air, and the heavy breaths of clubbers sticking to me….

It's okay, I tell myself. *It's okay.*

I'll shower when I get home, of course I will. No matter how sick I'm feeling, no matter how much my head is pounding and my stomach's churning. No matter how much my swollen, aching knees and lower back are begging me to just sit down for a moment, I won't because I will shower first.

But you won't be able to get your phone from your bag without washing your hands first.

I ignore that thought. The OCD. It's controlling, as always. Even out here. Even when I know I'm going to shower and thoroughly decontaminate myself.

I squeeze through dancing bodies, wincing with every accidental contact I make, and then I'm outside.

We're outside. The man grins at me, leans against the wall, tells me his name is Rob.

Well, I think his name is Rob. My ears are still ringing and there's a low roaring filling my head. Could've been Bob. Bob—nah, that sounds too old for a man this young. I take a deep breath. We're the only ones out here. Jana's not here. My gaze goes back to the door of the club. She must still be in there.

"So," Rob says. "Nice evening."

"Y-y-y…yes," I say, cringing at my usual speech problems. The sounds just get stuck in my mouth. Or sometimes they don't even get to my mouth; I often can't seem to translate what I'm thinking into words. But, at least here, I'll just sound like I'm drunk. This man won't know I've got a severe chronic illness. He's just Rob. Rob the… I try to work out what his character would be in my cartoon. Rob the Robber? Nah, that's silly. Rob the… But I don't know what he's like, whether he's a good guy or not, and that's important in my characters' names.

Unless I do run with that name. Rob the Robber. Make him a bad guy.

My eyes fall on a puddle of vomit near his feet. Revulsion pulls through me, and my skin starts to crawl. The OCD tries to tell me that the vomit's on me, that somehow particles of it are in the air and now are clinging to me. I try to ignore the voice as best as I can.

Rob the Robber must see me staring at the vomit, because he grunts and steps away. "It's those kids nowadays, they don't know how to hold their drink."

I look back at his face. Out here, in the near dark with one flickering streetlight, he looks more human, but older too. Late thirties? My stomach does a little flutter at that.

I hold onto my bag tighter—the little clutch bag I only ever use for this sort of stuff. Parties. Clubs. The things that aren't me at all. Inside my clutch bag is a jiffy bag with my phone, keys, ID, meds, and debit card in it. Couldn't put them straight in my bag. The OCD told me that'd be too dangerous.

Rob steps closer.

"What are you doing?" Alarm fills my voice.

He gives me a strange look. "Uh, how are we going to hookup if we stay ten feet apart?"

I step back. The back of my arm catches the rough brick wall, and I flinch. My sudden movement sends a serpent of pain down my left leg. "I'm not having sex with you." Or doing anything with him! Is…is that what he thinks is going to happen?

He looks around. "Yeah, s'pose it's not the nicest. We can go back to mine. Come on."

"Uh… no." I swallow hard. My eyes feel strange. This can't be happening. It *can't* be.

Rob's eyes narrow. "You've been leading me on?"

Leading him on? What the hell? I hadn't even danced with him—or even met him five minutes ago.

But you did agree to come out here with him.

I look back to the club. I need to get back inside there. Need to find Jana and Anastacia and her friends. Not be out here alone with this man. And it's not like we're at the front of the club, on the road with easy getaway access. We're at the back. A secluded vomit-splattered patio. "I don't go back to people's houses," I say.

"*People's* houses." He snorts. His tone becomes slightly menacing. "I'm not people."

"I don't do this sort of stuff though." My fingers are ice-cold. I take a step toward the door.

"Ah, you can have a bit of fun," he says. "Come on, we're both attracted to each other. You wouldn't have come out here with me otherwise."

I am not attracted to him—not at all, and especially not sexually. But there's no way I'm telling him that—or that I'm ace. He could flip out on me; it's happened before. I've got to put my safety first.

This was a bad idea. How stupid was I to think all going to a club was a good idea? Not just with my OCD but with being on the asexual spectrum too?

"Clubs aren't just for finding hookups," Jana had said earlier when I'd expressed doubt. "They're for having fun." And she's always saying I need to have more fun. My stomach tightens. I wonder if she agrees with those comments left on my profile—that I'm boring.

And maybe I do need to have more fun, because my life is just one hospital appointment after another, one episode of OCD after another, one crying session after another.

But looking at Rob now, with that glint in his eye, makes me wonder what exactly I've let myself into by coming out to "have fun."

My throat feels too thick and my mouth too dry, and suddenly I'm thinking about the woman who went missing two weeks ago. Marnie Wathem, a nineteen-year-old disappeared when walking some dogs. She's the talk of the town, and most people are saying she's just a runaway. That's the stance the cops have taken too; it's easier to believe nothing bad happens in Brackerwood, and also gives the police less work. But Marnie's brother has been adamant the whole time that she was abducted—or worse. He tried to get media attention on his views to prompt the police to do something, but that didn't work.

And I think he could be onto something. I mean, I read a lot of crime fiction, and so many of those books start with a similar situation where the town doesn't even realize a crime has taken place until it's too late. So many nights recently, I've thought about Marnie, let my half-dreaming brain conjure up all sorts of scenarios where, somehow, I'm the one who saves her.

But now, with Rob in front of me, I know I wouldn't be brave enough to save Marnie. I'm shaking so much, and I'm freezing up.

"I'm sorry, I can't do this," I say, trying to keep my voice as unconfrontational as possible. Because bad things can happen anywhere. Was Marnie really abducted? And my head is spinning and suddenly I'm convinced that the man in front of me is responsible.

I'm going to be his second victim.

But then Rob nods. "Okay."

He kicks at the gravel to the side of the patio, watches the stones cascade across the concrete slabs beyond, and then heads back to the club.

I breathe out a huge sigh of relief and follow. My heart pounds—did I really just avoid a dangerous situation or was that just my imagination? Hot air blasts back over me, and the music seems even louder than before. Rob's gone, disappeared into a mass of bodies, and I hold my bag close, my fingers shaking as I search for my friend.

"Jana!" I find her by the DJ, where the music's the loudest and most deafening. She looks bored as she stares at a couple who are making out.

With a jolt, I realize that the guy in the embrace is Jana's ex, Max. And the girl is Anastacia, her cousin. Wow. Anastacia the *Awful.*

"You ready to go?" Jana asks me, her eyes brightening. She twists the black ring on her finger.

"I nod. Let's get out of here," I say, looking around again in case Rob's watching. I can't see him. My stomach feels empty and slimy, and it's making me feel sicker now—both because of my illness, my medications, and the situation I narrowly avoided—but I also know I haven't eaten in a while. "We can get takeaway."

I know Jana's always up for chips, especially when she's had a drink or few. And I need to take my night-time meds, I should've already had them by this hour, and they have to be taken with food.

We say goodbye to Anastacia—not that she unlocks herself from Max's lips long enough to speak—and head out.

"I can't believe her," Jana says as we exit the club and step out into the high street. "She just *launched* herself at him…"

I make sympathetic noises—or, at least, I think I do. But I can tell my reactions are slow, and maybe they're so slow they don't leave my mouth at all. Because my mind is still on Rob.

What if he hadn't accepted no for an answer?

No, don't think of that. You're safe. Nothing happened.

"And he didn't exactly put up much of a fight, did he?" Jana huffs. "God, he can't even keep it in his pants. I was stupid to think he was ever okay with me being ace."

"Because that's what he told you," I say, and I have to concentrate on each word. I think I sound very drunk. "But don't think about that now."

She exhales sharply, digging a cigarette and lighter out of her bag. She checks which way the wind's blowing before lighting it—so the smoke won't blow over me, she's always very particular about that—and then swears loudly. About Max.

I do my best to pacify her, but the heaviness is taking over my body again. That and the OCD is picking up. Even though the smoke isn't directly going over me, I imagine it as a dusty blanket settling on my skin and dress and bag and hair.

You'll never get it out, the OCD whispers.

I try to ignore it. Focus on my surroundings—the streetlights, the red taillights of cars, the crisp, night air. On how even *if* there is smoke on me, it won't do me any harm. That's what my therapist says. And the psychiatrist too. And, anyway, I'm showering as soon as I get home. And then I can grab my graphics tablet and work some more on my cartoon strip to calm me before I sleep. I could draw some new caricatures. Maybe Jana. She features regularly in my art. Jana the Jewel, one of the main characters of my story. But she could be Jana the…Jazzy, too?

We pass a streetlight with one of the missing posters for Marnie Wathem tacked onto it. Her pale blue eyes set in her pale face seem to latch onto me as we walk past, and even once we're a block away from that poster, I still feel like the missing woman's watching me. It makes me shudder.

The chip shop is in sight now, and there's a man coming out of it, hands in his pockets, looking all casual and nonchalant. But there's something familiar about him, about the way his blond hair flops over his face. How he walks with confidence, but he also manages to look casual too.

"Is that…?" I stop, squinting ahead.

"What?" Jana asks with a grunt.

It's Damien. I inhale sharply. Damien Noelle. My eyes widen.

He hasn't seen me, and my heart's pounding, and I'm glad he hasn't seen me. So glad. My knees weaken, and I'm nervous—*of course* I'm nervous.

It's *him*.

My palms are sweating, and suddenly, it's like I'm back there, three years ago in Mallorca, on the retreat for those on the asexual spectrum, watching Damien Noelle make eye contact with me across the room. Eye contact that makes me giddy. Because he's *hot*.

Flashes of the rest of the two weeks and the time afterward fill my mind: Damien and me talking; Damien and me lounging in the games room; Damien telling me we'd have to meet up again back in England; Damien writing his number on the inside page of the book I was reading; me being too shy to call at first, and then realizing I'd lost the book when I was finally about to pick up my phone.

I swallow hard. How can he *be* here? I mean, what are the chances? The one guy I've been dreaming of bumping into again, more often than I'd like to admit, is *here*.

A numbness travels down the back of my right thigh.

"Nah, no one," I say, because if I tell Jana it's him, she'll make me go over and see him. Make me *talk* to him. And I can't talk to guys I like. I mean, sure I talked to Damien on the retreat, but that felt different. In Mallorca, I could almost be someone else. Someone confident. But here, I'm not confident. Not with guys. I'm shy and awkward. And I can't have Jana forcing me to go and talk to him, even if she thinks she's helping me.

Or Jana will have completely forgotten who he is. It's been three years, after all. Just because I think about Damien almost every day—regretting that I didn't decide to call him sooner—doesn't mean Jana will even remember him. I mean, most of the time on the retreat she was with Ray, a guy who's graysexual like her.

Unlike my relationship—if you could even call what Damien and I had on the retreat a 'relationship'—Jana's had survived the plane journey back. Ray lived in the midlands and they'd ended up in a long-distance relationship for a year after the retreat until they realized neither was willing to relocate. Jana has to stay in the area as she looks after her sister's kids when her sister's at work. And it was shortly after that breakup that she met Max the Moron, a straight guy who told her he was fine with her being on the ace spectrum.

But he wasn't.

Still, at least she's *had* relationships.

I haven't. Not one. I'm twenty-five and I've never been kissed—even if at several points on that retreat, I'd thought that Damien and I would. But we were both nervous, both cautiously dancing around each other, trying to figure each other out.

My eyes linger on Damien as he walks away. I breathe a sigh of relief. He didn't see me.

TWO

Damien

"HI EVERYONE," I say, and my voice catches a bit. Shoot, I sound nervous. So much for the confident tone I practiced on the drive to the airport—or on the plane, much to the amusement of the elderly couple next to me. But I explained to them where I was going and by the end of the flight they seemed more invested in making me appear like I wasn't anxious than I was. "Well, I'm Damien. Damien Noelle."

I suppress a smile. Roger from football told me to never introduce myself with my last name, not when I'm trying to meet girls as I've got a last name that sounds girlie, he says.

"And I'm a dog-walker," I finish.

The two women sitting together on the other side of the room make simpering noises.

"Wonderful," Mrs. Mitchell says. She's the organizer. A small, stout woman with a red face who greeted me with the warmest hug imaginable the moment I arrived. I half wondered if she had radiators under her jacket.

We're in a large conference room of the hotel, and this is the introductory session for all of those on this retreat. I'd thought it would be a bit tacky at first, and maybe it is, but it's nice to be around other people who get what being ace is like. Before today's introductory session,

I got chatting to a couple of the guys and they seemed cool enough. One of them says there's a table tennis table outside, overlooking the sea, and a bunch of us are going to meet for a game later.

I look at the two girls opposite. One's got black hair and one's a brunette with subtle honey highlights. The brunette keeps looking over my way. And she's cute. I can see that immediately. She laughs a lot with her friend, and I find myself wondering if they'd like to play table tennis too. They seem friendly.

"And would you like to tell us a bit more about you?" Mrs. Mitchell prompts.

"Of course." I clear my throat. Getting distracted already—that happens a lot. I like observing people, especially interesting people. Any kind of person, really. People I'd want to be friends with. People I'd want to avoid. People are just so fascinating.

"So, I'm probably demisexual," I say, because I assume that is what she means by her question. Now I wonder if volunteering to go first with introductions was wise. "I mean, I think I am demi?" Oh, God, I can feel myself panicking—and I always do, always worry that I'm using the words incorrectly or something. "I mean… I think so? Like, that's probably the word that best describes me, though sometimes I think gray might be better. But then I get all worried that I've been using the wrong one—even if demi does seem right at times."

"Hey, that's perfectly valid," Mrs. Mitchell says, "labels can and do change. It's not a cut-and-dried thing." She smiles. "And how about a boring fact about you?"

"A boring fact about me?" I look around, from face to face, all focused on me. And I can't think of a single thing. Oh, God, I'm so boring I don't even have a boring fact. I look down at my feet. "I'm wearing shoes that need repairing," I blurt out. "The left one, it's got a hole in it. But it's my favorite pair."

There are soft murmurs all around, and then Mrs. Mitchell is clapping her hands and everyone else tentatively joins in, before the man next to me is asked to go next. Apparently, we're going clockwise around the circle now.

"Okay, I'm Donnie," he says. He's sweating a lot, clutching his hands together in his lap. Looks nervous. Poor bloke. Got to be the oldest here too. In his sixties, I'd say. "Donnie Hamilton. And I'm an accountant."

As he talks about his accountancy and his business and his children and his ex-wife and how he left her for a man, who then left him, I'm counting round the circle until I get to the young women. Six people to go before I find out the name of the brunette woman.

"You're aromantic?" David, one of the men I spoke to earlier, says with a frown, jolting me back to the conversation.

"Yeah, I'm aromantic and graysexual." The fourth man is introducing himself. One of them whom I'm going to play table tennis with later. Ray, I think his name is.

"Why are you on a dating retreat then?" David asks. "If you're aromantic?"

"Aromantic people can have partners too," Mrs. Mitchell says. "Many do."

David grunts, looking bewildered. "I'm all so new to this."

"Yes, why don't you introduce yourself then?"

David does—he's a forty-one-year-old car mechanic who's never been married, never had kids, never learned the skillful art of tact, and is absolutely sure that he's going to find 'the one' on this retreat—and then at last it's the brunette woman's turn.

"I'm Cara," she says. "I'm… I've just left uni. I want to go into illustration. Haven't got a job yet though. And I'm ace and romantic. And a boring fact about me… I hate the texture of carpet. Can't walk barefoot on it."

"So, you'll always want to be wearing shoes then," Mrs. Mitchell says with a laugh. "Better make sure they haven't got holes in like Damien's."

I feel my face heat up. God, why did I talk about my broken shoes? But Cara is smiling at me, and her smile lights up her whole face.

I smile back.

"And your turn?" Mrs. Mitchell says, nodding her head toward Cara's friend.

The two of them arrived together at the hotel, last night. I was in my room, unpacking, when I saw them through the window. And I assumed then that they wouldn't be part of the ace retreat, because the hotel is huge, but then they turned up here.

"Jana," the friend says, and I wonder if they are together. Cara and Jana. Cara said she was ace and romantic but not who she's attracted to. Then again, I didn't specify I'm heterodemisexual either.

Jana continues her introduction, but I can't concentrate on what she's saying. I just want to talk to Cara.

THREE

Jana

MY ROOMMATE IS drunk and in a mood with me when I return. It's 2 A.M., I've just walked Cara back to her house, and River's glaring at me.

"I still can't believe that bitch didn't invite me," she says, her Devon-farmer accent thicker than normal.

River and Anastacia are always falling out. They have been ever since we were at school together. Many a morning would be spent with me going between their groups in the playground, trying to be both their friends on the days when the two of them weren't speaking.

"It wasn't even that great anyway," I tell her.

River shrugs and grabs another can. There are already several empty ones on the coffee table. She pushes back her dark hair—it's braided in two long plaits—and then flings her free hand out in a dramatic motion. "And I can't believe you went out with her."

"I wasn't just with her," I say. "Cara was there too. And some others."

"Lizzy and Phia?" River asks.

I shake my head. They'd both cancelled. Lizzy because she was behind with her studies and Phia because her sister wasn't well and she wanted to stay and look after her.

River grunts. "So, Cara goes out clubbing with you now, but doesn't come to our girly nights?"

"I had to beg her," I say.

River grunts again. "I don't think she likes me."

"Oh, come on, everyone likes you!"

"Not everyone—Anastacia, for example."

"Yeah but she falls out with everyone. And she got with Max tonight."

"Max as in your ex?" River nearly drops her can.

I nod. "I still can't believe it."

She swears. "Girl, you need to get revenge."

"Girl, I know," I say.

"Girl, what you going to do?"

"Girl, I don't know."

Starting each sentence with 'Girl' is something that dates back from our school days. We thought it was hilarious—Cara, Lizzy, Phia, and our other friends too. It was our thing, something that cemented our friendship. Now, it almost feels tacky when we do it—but we still say it. Me and River. Just every now and again.

"Come on, let's just get to bed," I say.

"You working tomorrow?" River asks.

"Afternoon shift," I say. And just thinking about work makes my stomach curdle and all its contents feel way too heavy. Lizzy and Phia are both on-shift in the morning too tomorrow. It used to be the three of us working the same shifts all the time, when Mr. Richards still ran his café, *The Red Panda,* on part-time hours. But last week he decided it would be full-time hours and instead of getting in more staff, he redid the rota. Sure, we all get more hours now—and more pay—but I don't like the thought of Lizzy and Phia being there alone with him. He's a greedy, racist, sexist shark. And there's safety in numbers.

FOUR

Cara

I STARE AT my face in the bathroom mirror. The dark circles under my eyes are no bigger than usual, even after last night, and my eyes themselves are dim. My skin is a sallow, off-white color. My hair is lank, dull, still damp from my shower when I got back in last night. Or rather the early hours of this morning.

Mum hadn't been pleased about how late it was. Bless her, she'd stayed up until I was back—only to tell me how I'd no doubt have made myself worse.

But I've proved I'm not boring.

I have a headache, the kind that feels like it's weighing down one side of my face. It can't be from the drink, because I only stuck to soft drinks. Can't have alcohol when I'm on these antibiotics. The guy at the bar at the back of the club had given me a bit of an odd look when I asked which soft drinks they had—like, *what are you doing at the club if you can't drink?*—but, oh well.

I shake off that feeling of being different—but of course it's not that which is making me uneasy. It's the OCD, as usual. My monster.

I'm okay, I tell myself. I'm clean—even if my OCD is a simmering pot, just waiting to suddenly boil over at the slightest thing. I'm fine.

I look around my room. It's getting messy in here again—my caricature sketches of River the Repulsive are spilling off my desk, along with pencils and pens. Some of the drawings of River are more than a little mean, but she doesn't know about them—only Raymond and Jana know about my cartoon. I struggle tidying my room though—everything feels too dirty to touch, and the pencils on the floor, I'm ashamed to admit they've been there a long while. I can't just put them back on the desk though. It's too dangerous.

And no one really gets it. Well, no one apart from Raymond. Except from Jana, he's the friend I talk to most. We met through an online support group for those with OCD caused by Lyme disease, and we quickly became friends. It was a relief to be able to talk to someone else who understands it all, because as much as Jana and Mum and my younger sister Esme all try to understand, they can't. That's the thing—you never really get it until you literally *get it.* It's part of the problem about the stigma around any chronic illness and mental health too. It's inaccessible for those who don't have it, and it leads to a lot of harm when people don't understand.

I want to write a book about it one day. I mean, Jana says I should. She writes a lot, and though I love reading—especially crime fiction—I'm more into drawing my cartoon. Maybe I'll do a cartoon about it.

"Ah, there you are," Mum says as I emerge from the bathroom, making sure to open the door with my foot—I never shut the door fully anymore, and I definitely never lock it, because then I'd have to use the handle. Just nudge it to with my foot. Mum, Dad, and Esme know to shout first before going into the bathroom now. "Can you take Riley for his appointment?"

Riley. I freeze. Our dog. The dog I can't touch.

"I know it's difficult," Mum says, "but I need to take Esme to the doctors. She's got bad earache again. And I'm sorry because I know you'll be tired after last night, but there's no way round it."

"Esme has earache again?" There's more than one reason my sister is Esme the Earache in my cartoon.

Mum nods. "And I don't want to cancel Riley's appointment. Hard enough to get them as it is. And your dad's got delayed."

"What? How long for?" I ask.

"He doesn't know. But he didn't get back at six this morning. Said it could be this afternoon but most likely later."

My eyes fall on the family photo wall. The snapshots of us when we were a happy family. So many memories. Me, grinning in my cross-country kit as I'm awarded a medal. Esme in her dance costume. The four of us dressed up all glam for a wedding. Mum and Dad laughing, their faces pressed close together. All four of us at the beach with Riley.

So many photos. So much happiness—but that's the *before.*

Dad works as a long-distance lorry driver now. We only see him a few days a week, if that.

"Don't worry," Mum adds, giving me a smile that's supposed to be bright and cheery but just has my stomach turning. "Riley will be a good boy, and he does like you. He'll be pleased to spend time with you again."

I know she doesn't mean to make me feel bad, but of course I do. Riley used to be my dog, years ago, before I got the OCD that told me he's contaminated, that made me afraid of him. Then he became Mum and Dad's dog, and I'd cry at night as I felt awful for abandoning him. Riley doesn't understand my OCD—hell, my parents can't even truly understand it—and it's not like I can explain to him why I suddenly stopped being available for pets.

Nausea is squeezing me now, and I can't tell whether it's fueled by my OCD or the antibiotics. Doxycycline always makes me nauseous. I swallow hard. My mind's already racing.

If you've got to do take the dog, there's a safe way. Wear different clothes. Don't take a bag. Minimize things that could get contaminated. Tie your hair up. Wear gloves. Avoid touching Riley as much as you can. And shower when you get back.

"Okay," I say.

The vet practice is on a little lane at the end of town, a twenty-minute walk from our house. I'm not allowed to drive because of the fainting, and how far I can walk without becoming ill varies day by day. I should've realized this morning would be worse, given how late I was out last night. By the time I'm a few minutes away, my breathing is labored and my legs feel too heavy. The sunlight's too bright now—even though I know it's not really, it's just my photosensitivity, made worse by the Doxycycline. Dizziness keeps coming for me in waves and that just makes me more scared—if I faint and fall on the ground, I'll be even more contaminated than I already am. I am really regretting refusing the lift that Mum offered me at the last minute. I was scared back at the house. I don't like getting in cars because of my OCD; you never know who else Mum has been offering lifts to. I don't like sitting on chairs outside the house—and in the house, there's only one that I feel safe on. One I cover up with a blanket when I'm not using it.

I'm wearing waterproof trousers over my leggings and wellies, my huge raincoat, and blue sterile gloves. Under my wellies, I've got on my wellington socks as I was too scared about my leggings and ordinary socks touching the inside of my wellies. Have to cover myself up as much as possible. My outfit rustles like a plastic bag with every step. Riley's a little wary of the noise and keeps as far away from me as he can on the leash. I feel bad, but I also feel safer.

Usually, when I walk into town, I listen to one of my audiobooks. I'm halfway through *Luckiest Girl Alive* by Jessica Knoll, and I'm just at a really disturbing part of it—I like dark, disturbing books. Jana is always horrified by my reading tastes. She's into contemporary romance and family saga. And anything with sex in it too—but not really erotic stuff, she told me once, there's got to be emotion in it too.

I'm more drawn to dark stories that tell you a lot about human nature. And I love an unreliable narrator. But I decide against listening to more of *Luckiest Girl Alive* now. It's too dangerous with Riley so close to me. He might knock my phone or my earphones or anything.

When the vets building is mere feet away, I breathe a sigh of relief. I can rest inside—even if I can't manage to sit down, standing still will help, won't it?

It won't help with the POTS.

And I want to curse that I have POTS—Postural Orthostatic Tachycardia Syndrome, the disorder that means my heart rate is way too fast. And standing still makes that worse. Makes me dizzier and faint

But I can't sit down when I get there. I'll have to keep pumping my calf muscles instead, try to keep my blood from pooling. I can rest properly when I get home. Having OCD as well as chronic illness just sucks.

The door opens, and a man steps out, right toward me—we're going to crash.

I jolt back and—

"Damien?" I stare at him.

It *is* him. Again. Looking so…amazing. I can't even think of a word other than 'amazing.' Blame the brain fog.

But Damien *is* amazing. And my heart does all these little fluttery things as I recall the retreat. Damien the Dashing—he has to be in my cartoon. Why isn't he already in my cartoon?

Damien looks up at me. His eyes widen a little. "Uh, Cara?"

A warm feeling fills my chest, and I'm trying not to smile too much because there's a chance I'll turn full-on into the Cheshire Cat. He *remembers* me.

"Hi." My voice is breathy, and Damien's giving me that easy smile that he gave to me so many times on that retreat, three years ago. My heart does a few more little fluttery jumps, makes me feel sicker with nerves. And I am sweating—sweating like a pig. So unattractive.

"Hi yourself." Damien leans forward, smiling. "And who is this?" He crouches down, fussing over Riley who of course decides that he absolutely loves Damien instantly. Or maybe he just wants some attention. I've avoided touching him pretty much from the moment Mum handed me his leash earlier.

God, I really hate the OCD.

"He's called Riley," I say.

"Well, Riley, you're looking like an extra good boy today." He looks up at me. "Is it a routine appointment?"

"Jabs," I say.

Damien nods. Then my throat squeezes. Damien came out of the vet practice without an animal.

Does that mean?

No—he could've been picking up medication or anything.

"I thought I saw you last night," I say, looking down at his head. He's still fussing over my dog, and I stare at Damien's hair. Messy, dark blond. Shorter than it was three years ago. Then he could tie it in a ponytail, but I think it's slightly too short for that now. "Coming out the takeaway on George Street? I didn't think it could be you, like I thought you lived in Dorset, but I guess it was you?"

He laughs and looks up. "Yep, that was me. Do love a good curry and chips. Didn't see you though." He plays with Riley some more, stroking all the silky hair around Riley's ears. Riley who's now trying to lick Damien. "Yeah, I've just moved here—was just dropping cards off here." He gestures toward the door of the vet. "Business cards. I'm a dog-walker."

I step back a little, extending the lead. "I remember."

Damien squints up at me, and I study his face, try to imprint it into my memory even more, ready to draw later. Those blue eyes, the square jaw, the narrow nose, the dark blond hair that's slightly wavy.

"Aren't you hot with all those layers on?" he asks.

I sure am, and I know my face is red and sweaty, but I shake my head. I can't take any of the layers off anyway. Not out here.

"I've got to get him inside," I say. "Don't want to be late."

"Ah, okay," Damien says. He's still smiling at Riley, but then he glances at me. "Nice to see you, though. And you and Riley will have to show me the best walks around here. Don't want to disappoint any of my clients."

"Sure," I say, even though the OCD is telling me that's never going to happen. I'm not going for a walk with Damien and Riley. I can't. It's too dangerous, being near so much contamination. And if Damien's walking other people's dogs, he is going to be covered in all sorts of dog hair and particles and bad stuff.

But if you don't go, you'll regret it… You'll prove River right again. Because if you go on a date, you can't be boring.

Damien pulls out a business card from his pocket. "My number's on that—if you want to call me."

He's holding the card out and I have to take it, and I don't want to touch it, even though I've got gloves on. But I have to.

I take it gingerly. *Damien Noelle. Professional dog-walker, qualified in dog first-aid. Can walk dogs alone or in groups.*

"See you then," he says, turning away.

"See you," I echo, and I feel sick as I head into the vet.

FIVE

Damien

I GAVE CARA my number. Again—didn't the first time teach me the lesson? What the hell was I thinking? I groan as I walk back home. How desperate did I come across? As if I am still pining for her after three years? Three years since I gave her my number and she never called me. Hell, did she even look pleased to see me?

I swallow hard, feeling my face get redder and redder. Oh, God. She's going to think I've been waiting for her call all these years. And that I'm not getting her hints.

But I *have* been thinking about her all this time. You don't spend two weeks with someone like Cara—someone who you just click so well with—and then not think about them.

"Snap out of it," I tell myself—because I'm one of those people who talks to himself too. Ha. Maybe that's why she wasn't interested in me after all.

My new apartment isn't far away, and by the time my key is in the door, I've got about an hour until my first appointment. An elderly lady living in the same block of flats wants me to walk her golden retriever. She phoned me last night, mere hours after I'd moved in. I hadn't had a chance to get any of my cards out anywhere, but I'd talked to a bloke in the foyer by the lift as I was waiting for the removals company and told him what I do. Guess news travels fast.

Cody, my new roommate, is sitting at the kitchen table. He looks up and gives me a grunt by way of a greeting. First thing he told me on the phone when I inquired about the spare room he was letting out was that he wasn't much of a talker. I'd laughed goodhumoredly until his second sentence had been, "So I'm going to text for the rest of this conversation." Sure enough, he'd hung up straight away, and moments later had sent a follow-up text.

In person, he's no more talkative. Barely got two words out of him last night—and those were in response to me saying I was going out to get takeaway and asking if he wanted any. I'd meant it as a roommate-bonding thing, but he'd taken his dinner into his room and shut the door the moment I'd returned with the hot food.

"I'm only back for an hour or so," I say, because Lord help me—I have to talk to someone. I'm just one of those people.

Cody nods. He's got a short hairstyle that emphasizes how bony his skull is at the back, and I can't help but think longer hair would look better on him. The newspaper's spread out in front of him, and I lean over as a headline catches my attention: *Local Dog-Walker Still Missing.*

"Whoa, is that round here?" I ask.

Cody doesn't answer, but I'm already reading.

Nineteen-year-old student Marnie Wathem is still missing since 10 P.M on September 12th, when she failed to return home. In the two weeks since, there have been no new developments, and Detective Matthews has announced that Wathem's disappearance is not suspicious. "Marnie is known as a bit of a terror," he told us. "She wanted to run away, and we have no reason to think another person is involved."

Wathem's brother, Trevor Wathem, 31, said his sister had been out walking a group of dogs—part of her new business efforts to save up for the university course she wanted to do, after she'd left her job as a waitress three months ago—but had not returned. He says his sister "would never abandon the dogs like that," and says he believes the police are wrong in their assumption that the young woman is simply a runaway. The four dogs Wathem was walking were all found in the early hours of the next morning, barking and causing riot amid a field of sheep over on Westford Common. The farmer, Mr. John—

Cody turns the page.

"Hey," I say. "Can I just read that?"

Cody's dark, soulful eyes turn to me. He shakes his head. "My paper. Get your own."

If I wasn't so interested in the report, I'd be marveling at his use of actual words.

"Come on, man," I say. "There was only one paragraph left."

Cody gets up, folds the newspaper, and places it against his heart before leaving the kitchen.

I shake my head as I watch him go, then pull out my phone. "Marnie Wathem," I mutter as I type her name into Google. There are a lot of articles about her disappearance, but none of them give any more actual info about why she disappeared. Just interviews with the farmer whose sheep were hurt by the dogs, mostly. There aren't even any photos of the missing woman.

"Always was trouble, that girl," Mrs. East says as I collect Rufus, her golden retriever. "She never was reliable."

"But she's gone *missing*," I say. You can't say these sorts of things about a missing woman. Who knows what's happened to her?

"She hated doing this job anyway, was only in it for the money," Mrs. East continues as if she didn't hear me. Maybe she didn't. Her hearing aid is making a lot of squeaking noises.

There's not really much I can say to that, and something tells me that this lady is not one to be argued with. So, I say goodbye, trying not to roll my eyes as she tells her dog that she'll have his roast chicken dinner waiting for him when we get back. I'm not entirely sure whether she expects me to take Rufus on a walk longer than the forty-five minute one she's booked me for, especially if she's cooking from scratch.

"Come on, boy," I say. Rufus walks in a way that my mum would call 'pudgily.' He's definitely had one too many roast dinners with all the trimmings before, in my opinion.

We head out into the woodland to the north of Brackerwood. Mrs. East was very particular about the places where her precious boy is walked, and told me that there are eight different routes Rufus likes, and he gets moody if you try and take him anywhere else. She'd told me to take him on tis walk specifically.

"It's one of his favorites," she had said to me with a beam.

It's also the last walk that Marnie Wathem took the dogs on. The walk where she disappeared.

"Do you know what happened?" I ask Rufus, stopping at one point to stroke his head. "Did you see?"

I have a dark imagination. It's all the true crime documentaries and podcasts I surround myself with. I'm just fascinated by them, the murderers. It sounds bad to say, but they're one of the most interesting types of people. Not interesting in an entertaining way, interesting in a morbidly fascinating way. I'd wanted to study criminal psychology at uni at one point—back at the time when I thought I'd definitely be going to university, before my parents had declared bankruptcy and we'd had to move, uprooting me in the middle of my A-levels. My new school hadn't offered a psychology course and so I'd taken hard sciences instead—and failed.

But I'm still fascinated by criminals, especially serial killers. I want to know how their minds work. I want to explore their thought processes and what makes them think their actions are justified. Are serial killers really all psychopaths? Do they feel no remorse at all as they murder their victims?

And is a crime case like that what Marnie's been caught up in? Or is it an abduction case?

As I walk Rufus, I entertain the idea that maybe I'll be the one to find Marnie. Maybe she *has* been abducted and this route I'm taking will unlock the mystery of what happened to her. If I was the one to rescue her from some monster, then I'd be branded a hero. And if I was a hero, I'd get attention, for sure. Maybe Cara would be interested in me because of said heroism.

I groan. "Man, why am I like this?" I bend down to ruffle the fur on Rufus's head. There's a tennis ball in my pocket, and it digs into me as I bend down. I'd planned on throwing it for him, but when I got it out upon leaving Mrs. East's house, Rufus looked at it disdainfully. "I need to just forget about Cara, don't I, boy?"

Rufus clearly couldn't care less, and he doesn't seem to be enjoying this walk—not in the way that other dogs I've walked before do. Hmm. Maybe he really did see something out here when Marnie disappeared. Or maybe he's not enjoying it because he's a bit overweight and not used to exercise. I mean, if he had seen something, he'd be anxious being back here, right?

"Here you go, my precious boy," Mrs. East practically whimpers as she has me pick Rufus up and place him on his seat at the table. His chair has a red, velvet cushion on.

Rufus eyes the plate of food—yep, a full roast chicken dinner, with way too much fat on the meat—on the table in front of him and licks his lips.

"Your money's on the counter," Mrs. East tells me without looking at me. "You can see yourself out."

My stomach rumbles at the aromas of the food as I collect the two notes and leave.

Walking back to my new place—I still can't bring myself to call it 'home' yet—I check my phone for messages from any more prospective clients, or, by some miracle, Cara. There are none from either.

Cody does his silent I'm-going-to-pretend-you're-not-here act when I let myself back into the apartment, so I decide to do my own I'll-ignore-you-too routine. It's remarkably easy. I make a quick cup of tea, grab a couple of chocolate cookies, and head to my room. My box of crime books is on the floor, ready to be unpacked. I put my cup of tea on the windowsill, balance one of the cookies on the mug's rim, and pop the other in my mouth.

Then I set about unpacking my books.

This book collection is arguably something I'm most proud of. Dad called me pathetic once, for being so into reading, when he was angry one time that I didn't want to go to the park or play outside like the 'normal' kids. But taking out these important books makes me smile, makes me think it's a rebellious act against him. And, good. He's the reason Mum went bankrupt.

Mum had this amazing flower-arranging business that she'd built from scratch. Dad had a gambling problem. He spent all their life savings and then remortgaged Mum's shop without telling her, forging her signature. I'm not quite sure what happened after that—no one really told me or my brother—but two months later, we had to sell our house and the shop and move to a shoddy apartment. All of us. I still think Mum should've left Dad behind.

This box of books was the only thing I could take, and I carefully remove the volumes now and spread them out on my bed.

My phone buzzes. I pull it from my pocket.

It's an unknown number. A new client?

I click onto the text.

Hi, it's Cara. Do you want to meet tomorrow? I can show you some good walks.

My eyes widen. Cara. She's interested? That's what this has to mean, right?

A grin breaks across my face.

She's *interested.*

SIX

Cara

"I AM GOING to kill you." I stare at Esme the Earache then back at my phone. She touched my phone—actually *touched* it.

And no one's allowed to touch my phone. *I* can't even touch my phone sometimes.

My breaths come in ragged bursts, and my vision dims around the edges. My pounding heart seems to get faster and faster, and—oh, God! I'm going to faint. Going to fall on the floor—the *sticky* kitchen floor—and get more and more covered in….in bad stuff.

I take a deep breath. Need to pull myself together. Can't faint here. Can't panic.

But my precious *phone*!

I focus on what's on the screen. Damien's reply: *Wonderful, I'm in High Court Flats, meet outside them?* It's a reply to a text I most definitely did not send.

"Oh, come on, you've been mentioning him all slyly all day. And how he wanted you to show him round, then moaning about your OCD. Just get out there." Esme gives me a cheeky look.

"I thought you were supposed to be ill." I give her a look, but I feel strange—because that was why I was mentioning Damien, wasn't it? Because I like him. I definitely do. Seeing him again definitely taught me that.

"You can still help others when you're ill." There's something about how Esme's tone darkens that makes me think this is a dig at me. I've had Lyme disease for just under three years. Esme was ten years old when I got it, and for a long time, she refused to understand why I couldn't just play with her as I used to. Mum is always reminding her that my brain has now gone wrong, just like my body did, all because the tick that bit me had a disease.

"And you'll have fun," she says. "And then you'll get better."

I give her a weak smile, head up to my room, clean my phone four times, and then message Raymond. My fingers feel strange as I type, sort of buzzing from the inside. I flex them several times before hitting 'send' on the message.

You'll never guess what Esme's done?

What?

Only gone and set me up on a date!!!

There's a pause, in which I wait for his reply, but then my phone vibrates. Video call through Messenger. Raymond always prefers video. His Lyme disease makes his fingers inflamed which doesn't help his juvenile arthritis. Speaking is easier for him.

I have a moment of panic about how scruffy I look, and how messy my room is, before answering. Not like I can run a brush through my hair—add that to my list of OCD curses.

"Hi," Raymond says. His face fills my screen. He's Black, has red-tipped box braids and statement glasses that make him look so much cooler than me.

"Hey," I say, and my voice squeaks. I always get nervous speaking on video calls. Or any calls really—I find written word easier. I can take my time then to write an articulate answer—or an answer as articulate as I can manage—whereas speaking puts me on the spot. And sometimes it's okay—like now, my brain doesn't feel like it's fully of sludgy mud—but other times I can barely string a sentence together and then my voice betrays me when I actually try to speak.

"So, a date?" Raymond asks. "Who with? Spill!"

"Okay." I sit on the edge of my bed and hold my phone a little higher, trying to make the lighting on my camera better. "You remember me mentioning Damien?"

"Damien? As in Damien who you were too scared to text and then tragically lost his number? That Damien?"

"Yes." I quickly explain what Esme's done.

It's such a cliché to say, but I've definitely got butterflies in my stomach just thinking about the date tomorrow. The date with *Damien.*

Raymond's eyes are wide. "No way. You going to go?"

I swallow hard. My throat is a little sore—but that's nothing new. My lymph nodes are often swollen now. "I don't know—like, I'm terrified. Actually *terrified.*"

"But it would be good for you, right? You still like him?"

Of course I do. But it's complicated. It's not like I could have a relationship with him now or anything. And just the thought of it—of having to cuddle someone, and more—because he'll still want to kiss, won't he?

Even though we both identify as ace, it doesn't mean we're both never going to touch, if something were to happen between us. Asexuality is a spectrum, and it includes a whole host of different identities. A lot of aces kiss and touch and some have sex. I think of Jana. She's gray-ace and she's told me she does like sex, she just doesn't feel sexual attraction that often and when she does, it's low-intensity.

"I'm sort of halfway between being ace and allo," she'd said once. "Or maybe I'm closer to the ace end. I don't know."

All I'd known when she'd talked about it was that I was definitely not gray-ace. I've never actually felt sexual attraction, and now, with the added bonus of my OCD and contamination fears, the idea of doing anything at all makes my stomach twist. I can't even hug people platonically.

"I don't think I can go though," I tell Raymond, and my voice is all thick and wobbly. "My OCD. You know what it's like."

Raymond nods. "But sometimes you've got to try. That's what my therapist said to me when I was scared about dating again. And look at me now, with Ali."

Raymond met Ali a year ago. He's been ill with Lyme much longer than me, and in many ways, he's a step ahead of me in this game. But I remember his angst-ridden calls last year, when he'd told me he was really attracted to Ali and he'd never met anyone like her. For so long he believed that he'd just have to "let her go" and not make a move at all or let her know he was interested. He'd talked about it with his therapist, and we'd always talked about it after each of his therapy sessions too.

The first time Raymond told me he'd been able to hold Ali's hand without freaking out, he'd had the biggest grin on his face. Then he'd told me about the first hug, the first kiss, and more…until I'd stopped him, telling him I didn't want to know all the details. But he says that Ali's the only one he can touch now without panicking.

I wonder what it would be like if I could touch Damien without panicking. If he was the only one that my OCD became immune too. Then I think about Mum and Dad and Esme and Jana—the hurt they'd feel if they saw me hugging Damien when I still flinch around them. Because if I do manage to hug one person, I'm just so sure I won't be able to hug everyone.

"I'm really not sure I can do this though," I say. "And it's tomorrow—it's too short notice. I'll just have to text Damien and say I can't. I'll explain it was Esme texting and not me."

"But this is your chance, Cara," Raymond says, ever-rational. Most often, he even features in my cartoon as Raymond the Rational—which he loves, by the way. "And if you don't take it, you might not get another one. Come on, we can't let our illnesses hold us back."

"It's easy to say though."

"I know." The screen freezes for a moment but then Raymond's back. "But you don't want the OCD controlling another aspect of your life."

I sigh. My fingers are starting to cramp now from holding up my phone, and I see if I can balance it on my bedside table. "I know you're right…but it's just so scary."

Scary. I think of all the crime fiction I read. It's almost comical calling my life 'scary' compared to what some of those poor characters go through.

"I know," he says. "Trust me, I know. But I wouldn't be your friend if I wasn't trying to tell you to go for this. Just hope he's not a serial killer or anything, else I'm going to feel terrible for encouraging you to see him if that's the case." He laughs.

I like Raymond's laugh. It's rich and grounding. It reminds me of normality—my normality now—of talking to Raymond for hours on end. At first, when we met, virtually, we'd only talk about stuff to do with Lyme and OCD and the therapy sessions, but after a few months, we began sharing other details of our lives. I added him on Facebook and saw cute photos of his cocker spaniel, and he liked the odd photo I put up of Riley—the photos where I pretend to all my Facebook friends that everything is still normal and that I can still play with my dog.

We talk for maybe half an hour more, mainly with Raymond updating me on what he calls his "life plan." Once he's cured from Lyme disease—as much as anyone with chronic Lyme disease can be cured—he's going to get a job in the video-game industry. Raymond is amazing at drawing—I've seen some of his sketches—and he also loves storytelling. Before he became ill, he was going to study game development and become a professional games designer, and so that's what his plan is. He'll resume his planned life, once he's better.

"Then once we've saved up, Ali and I are going to travel around the world," he says. "We'll visit every country beginning with R and A—the first letters of our names, you know—and when we arrive at the last one, currently planned to be Azerbaijan, I'm going to ask her to marry me."

"What?" I stare at him, feel the gasp in my word like a physical tug of breath inside me. "Oh my god!" Excitement bubbles within me—it always does when anyone mentions proposal plans. Though I've never had a relationship, I love romantic stuff, and any kind of TV show about weddings is right up my alley. *Don't Tell the Bride* is currently my favorite. It's a bit of a contrast to my other favorite things—like crime fiction and true crime—and it often surprises people.

"Do you think it's tacky, though?" Raymond asks. "Proposing on vacation—and in the last country? We could both be really grouchy and tired."

"I think it's lovely," I say.

I wonder if anyone—Damien—will ever propose to me. Then that makes me think about the date tomorrow, and I swallow hard.

It's just a date.

I can do it.

I will.

Raymond's right—if I don't, I'll regret it. How often do second chances come around?

SEVEN

Cara

"WE HAVE TO get to the other side?" I stare at Damien. His face is flushed from the cool breeze, and it makes him look rugged. Like he's stepped right out of a survival program.

"Uh huh." He nods and narrows his eyes as he looks across the river—the far side has to be thirty or forty feet away. "And we're not allowed to swim, and we can't get wet."

A little line appears between his eyebrows as he frowns, and I'm struck by how cute that makes him look. A warm, glowing feeling fills me. It's the same feeling that filled me earlier, when Mrs. Mitchell divided us into pairs for this task. I'd assumed wrongly that we'd be able to choose them—of course I'd pick Jana—but when she said she'd already organized us into teams, I'd started to panic inside. Until I'd been paired with Damien, and he'd given me this little smile that somehow felt intimate and personal, just between the two of us, even though everyone else was milling about.

Now, all around us, the other competitors are jumping into action. Jana and her partner—a middle-aged woman called Freda—are talking furiously to my left. Jana's covering her hand with her mouth, like she always does when she doesn't want her idea to be copied. David and

Donnie have already headed back up the mountainside. I heard Donnie say they can cut down trees to make a boat. Huh, as if that's going to be the answer. This is a retreat, not a survival camp. And it would take days to make a boat, right? But the other eight couples are milling around, looking about as lost as Damien and me.

"So, we build a raft," I say. Because, let's face it, a raft is going to be much more practical and easier to build than a boat.

"With what?" Damien asks. "We've got no tools. We've got nothing."

As if on cue, I look around. There's a cooler a few feet behind me and Damien, containing bottles of water and bananas. "For energy," Mrs. Mitchell had said, before disappearing back into the bus and driving away. That's all we've got.

"Well, there has to be something obvious that we're missing." I shiver a little. I hadn't realized it would be so cold here. Didn't bring many layers or anything. Always thought Mallorca was supposed to be hot.

"Hey," a woman in her late thirties shouts. Bianca. "Anyone get any idea what to do?"

Jana and Freda keep on talking, looking all secretive and mysterious. There's a glint in Jana's eyes, one she only gets when she's plotting.

"No."

"No idea, mate."

"What's to stop us swimming anyway? Or wading? Mrs. Mitchell isn't even here."

"Because that's cheating," Damien says, and the way he says it just makes me like him more—because he doesn't want to cheat. He wants to do this properly. He wants our victory to be deserving—if, indeed, we do manage to win.

"Maybe we should all work together—all of us," another woman says.

"But we're divided into pairs," Jana says. "So only two can win. And we're going to win, me and Freda."

Damien laughs and meets my eyes. His are a pale blue, and I find myself feeling warmer—forgetting about the cool weather, even though his irises are a cool color—as I drink in those gorgeous eyes.

"We don't even know what the prize is," someone says.

"Doesn't matter." Damien smiles. "Winning is a reward in itself. And this—" He spreads his arms out. "This exercise is about having fun and getting to know your partner."

His eyes are still on me, and it's almost as if the others aren't here—because all I can concentrate on is Damien. I feel my face heating up as I smile, and I realize I'm stepping closer to him.

I just want to be close to him, and it surprises me because I've not felt like that before. But Damien's like a bright star in an icy night, and I'm magnetized toward him. And being close—close enough I can smell the slightly spicy tones of his aftershave—just makes me want to be around him more.

"So, what are we going to do?" His voice is low now, a whisper meant just for me as he steps closer to me still. Mere inches separate us. "Because no matter what I said, I do want the prize. I heard it's chocolate."

"Chocolate?" My mouth waters.

He nods, his eyes bright. "So, we need a plan. We've got to get across the river without swimming or getting wet."

I breathe deeply as I look across the river again. My head feels heavy, but a good kind of heavy, and I know it's because Damien's so close to me. I've never stood so close to a man before and not felt nervous—even at uni, I was just so awkward in seminars when I had to sit next to guys. I could barely say a word. I was too anxious. But, with Damien, it's easy. We've been talking and I haven't been panicking. It feels right.

I hope we're paired together for the next challenge too.

"Can you fly?" There's a mischievous glint in Damien's eyes.

"Alas, I left my wings at home."

"Shame. Me too." He laughs, a low, throaty sound now.

"Hold on." My eyes widen. "We only have to get to the other side of the river, right?"

He nods, inclining his head toward me slightly. He's about six inches taller than me, and he looks down at me with such tenderness that I nearly stop breathing.

"There's… There's nothing to say we have to cross right here," I whisper.

"Nothing to say a lot anyway." He pushes his hair back. Longish, blond hair. Then he retrieves a rubber band from his pocket, starts to tie it back.

"That's gonna pull your hair," I say, sliding my spare hair tie off my wrist. "Here."

"Thanks."

I wait until he's tied his hair back then I lower my voice again. "I'm sure there was a bridge—back there. We drove past it. On the bus."

His eyes widen. "Yes." His grin is huge. "So, we walk back there and cross on the bridge?"

"We do." I give him a nod.

"Well, I guess we better get wood and make this damn raft," he says in a loud voice, then winks at me—actually winks.

I find myself laughing as the two of us hurry away. And it feels almost magical walking away with Damien. Just me and him, going into the woodland. I flick a glance over my shoulder and see Jana watching me. She's probably regretful she got paired with Freda, because Damien is hot.

I almost want to laugh, thinking that. Because I've never thought that about anyone before. But Damien is hot. *Attractive. There's a carefree side to him that just makes me think he's never stressed. And he's strong, that's obvious in the way his jacket arms are straining across his biceps. He looks good. Very good.*

"So, you're from England, too, right?" Damien asks me.

"Yep. Devon," I say.

"Oh, fairly close to me then. I'm in Dorset." He holds back a branch that sticks out over the pathway, so I can get past it easily. "We'll have to meet up after this retreat then."

Meet up? My eyes widen, and my heart's doing all these little skipping things that make me feel even more giddy. Damien wants to meet up with me?

I feel my face redden even more. Is he interested in me? Like I'm interested in him—and I am interested, aren't I? Because he just seems so nice, and I want to know more about him. I want to know everything. The realization sends shock waves through me. I've not felt this yearning desire to know a person like this before. But I just want to be around him.

"Are you cold?" Damien asks, concern in his voice. "Here." He takes off his jacket, freeing those arms that are definitely very muscular—the kind of muscular that would have River drooling—and drapes the garment over my shoulders. The back of his hand brushes against my face, just for the tiniest fraction of a second.

"Thank you." I hardly dare to breathe, but then he's walking again.

"Come on. We've got to get to the other side first." He sounds determined—and I like that. Hell, I seem to like every single thing about him—how is that possible? This has never happened before.

I breathe deeply.

"Hey, do you think Donnie and David are going for the bridge too?" he asks.

My pace quickens. I hadn't thought of that.

"Guess we'd better run," I say.

Damien holds his hand out for me. I take it. Warmth—and it's not just from his jacket—floods through me at an alarming speed. He squeezes my hand. "Let's go."

And then we're running.

There's something special about running through the woods—through the middle of nowhere, it seems—with Damien. Our footsteps create our heartbeats, and he squeezes my hand firmly, with confidence.

We race through the trees.

"There it is!" I point with my free hand. The bridge.

Damien's panting, but we speed up more at the sight of it. Buzzing sensations fill me as we reach the bridge, and I'm looking around. Donnie and David, are they here?

"No one in sight," Damien says.

Our feet clang on the bridge, and we slow down just enough to look over it, at the river. The water swirls fifteen feet below. It's so clear I can see every stone on the riverbed.

Then we're running again. Adrenaline pounds through me, and I don't think my heart's ever beaten so fast, even on one of my cross-country runs.

We run and we run, and I watch the others as they come into sight on the original side of the river. Jana's mouth drops open.

"We did it!" I cry, and Damien's smiling.

I try to catch my breath. Damien's jacket smells of him, and I breathe in deeply. It sounds silly to say it makes me feel safe—but it does.

"Well done." Mrs. Mitchell steps out from behind a tree—actually behind a tree—and I jump. "We have our winners."

She hands us two bars of Galaxy chocolate.

Damien is laughing as he leans in close to me. "Told you," he whispers to me, that mischievous look on his face, the one that just makes my heart pound harder.

EIGHT

Jana

"I CAN'T BELIEVE he gets away with treating us like that," I mutter darkly. I can still hear Mr. Richards bellowing out there. Poor Lizzy.

"We should all do something," Phia says, taking her apron off. She hangs it on the peg at the side of the staff room—which is barely big enough for four people to stand in—and then shakes her glossy dark hair out. It's naturally black, but she recently dyed it a vibrant red, and she's totally rocking the look, despite what our boss thinks.

When Mr. Richards first saw Phia's new hair color he told her he didn't think Asian women should dye their hair as "it doesn't suit them" (whatever that means), and Phia and I told him exactly what we thought of that comment, earning ourselves written warnings. Not that the written warnings mean anything. He's not going to fire us, not when he went to so much trouble to hire the three of us specifically in the first place.

"Make a stand," Phia continues. She grabs her compact mirror from her bag and checks her make up. As usual, her winged eyeliner is perfect. I'm always jealous of how amazingly she can do it—and so quickly too. Phia snaps the mirror together. "He can't treat us like this."

"A stand? Like a strike?" I turn to her, nearly knocking her with my elbow.

"*And you think that's a way to speak to a customer!*" Mr. Richards's voice is loud, even through the door.

"*I wasn't going to be humiliated like that.*"

"*What happened to the customer is always right?*"

"What happened to the customer when he's a sexist pig?" I mutter. Because I'd been out serving the table next to Lizzy's when the incident happened. A guy in his thirties had grabbed Lizzy's behind. She'd told them to leave, at which point he'd asked for the manager. And of course Mr. Richards took the customer's side. Why would he ever want to protect one of the young women he'd hired? We all know we only got the job because of our looks—he made it clear in our interviews. Lizzy, Phia, and I started here together, right after the factory we all previously worked at closed. Mr. Richards had contacted our former bosses and asked for us specifically.

"Yes, I want some attractive young girls," he'd said. "Different races too, if I can. Don't want anyone accusing me of being racist." Apparently, that was why his last waitresses had left. All three of them—all white—had quit in protest after they'd heard him on the phone using racist language.

What. An. Asshole. Though hiring staff of different ethnicities doesn't mean he now can't be accused of being a racist. And given the words he mutters about Lizzy and Phia when he thinks we're out of earshot, he definitely still is. The two of them always end up bearing the brunt of his idiocy. I'm white, so he's a bit nicer to me. It makes my blood boil.

We should've known what we were getting ourselves into. I mean, we knew he was problematic from the start, and we were hesitant, but we didn't think Mr. Richards could be this bad. And we also needed jobs, and jobs aren't easy to find in Brackerwood. Most of the others I used to work with got work in the city, but I need to be close by so I can take care of my niece and nephew when needed. My sister's an on-call doctor and she doesn't get much warning a lot of the time.

So, the three of us accepted this job—just until we found something better, that was the plan. But now we're here, we're bonded even more. United in our hatred for Mr. Richards. And I can't just leave the other two to endure Mr. Richards on their own. We're a team. We always have been.

The unmistakable sound of Mr. Richards storming out of the café reaches us. Lizzy enters our room. Her eyes are watering, and she's blinking fast.

"Did you get anything?" I ask her. I take off my own wire. We ordered the kits cheaply, and they only pick up words from a few meters away, but the sound isn't always that clear. We need evidence if we're going to take down Mr. Richards. Using recording apps on our phones would be much better—if Mr. Richards even allowed us to have our phones on us during shift.

He doesn't. He said that the bulky shape of a phone in a pocket 'ruins' a woman's natural shape. Apparently, if we so much as hide our phones in our bras, we're violating the terms of our employment. Then he spent way too long leering at us and said he didn't want to have to introduce full body searches but he would if he suspected we had our phones on us.

"We better have," Lizzy says, unhooking her wire.

"Maybe we should get an undercover diner in," Phia says. "Like you see on those TV shows where horrible bosses are exposed."

"Like *Watchdog*?"

"Nah, that's more for scams," I say.

Phia shrugs and reaches for her coat. "We need someone to witness it—especially if these wires don't work."

And that's the thing. We've been wearing these for a week, and there were plenty things they should've picked up—but they didn't. The sound was too poor, too low quality. Words were muffled, and the whole sound was distorted, so much so that at a time when Mr. Richards was insulting Phia it didn't even sound like him. And of course he'd claim that it wasn't him if we ever tried to use it. Nah, we need indisputable proof.

"Maybe we should set up cameras too."

Lizzy's eyes widen. "I'm not happy wearing a wire in case he finds out. Cameras would be so much worse."

"We could disguise them."

They each hand me their memory cards. We'll listen to the audios we recorded later, as we sit in my apartment with River and eat ice cream and the brownies I baked a couple days ago.

"Too risky." Lizzy shakes her head, then lets down her locs. "We've got to be careful." She looks at me. "It's easier for you. If he catches you recording him, you'll just get a slap on the wrist."

She's right, I know she is, and it just makes my stomach tighten more.

We talk about it all for a few more minutes, until Phia complains about how slow her boyfriend is at replying to her texts from earlier, and that launches us into complaining about men—current partners and exes and the blokes that never notice us. A conversation that lasts us until we get to my apartment. River lets us in and tells us she's ordered takeaway to arrive in an hour.

"I still can't believe Max got off with Anastacia." I shake my head as we make our way into the living room and lounge on the sofas.

A few weeks ago, River found an advertisement on Facebook Marketplace for the most amazing set of sofas—free to a good home. They're proper luxury, and we snapped them up. Lizzy and I are on one, River and Phia on the other. The coffee table between us holds an array of different ice cream cartons and a handful of newspapers.

"How's Cara doing?" Lizzy asks. "She still not joining us?"

I shake my head. "I mean, she's still the same. But socializing is… It's difficult for her." I think of what she was like at the club. I could sense her unease. It just radiated off of her. I was surprised she'd even gone to be honest, especially when she only comes to our Tuesday Girls' Nights about once a month.

"Haven't seen her in ages." Phia shrugs.

It used to be us girls plus Cara and two others who now live in London, back in the day. We all went to school together.

Phia reaches for the nearest ice cream carton. Mint choc chip. She spoons some into her mouth, gets a smudge of it next to her lips on that oh-so-flawless skin of hers. Seriously, she has amazing skin. Out of our whole group, she's easily the hottest. And all the boys back at school confirmed that. It was Phia who they all wanted to go out with. River only joined the club once her bra-size increased.

For the last few years of school, the boys were chasing Phia and River, and the rest of us rarely got a look-in. Apparently, I was too bossy and Cara was too shy. Lizzy's parents were strict and never let her have a boyfriend, but then Lizzy was more into gaming at that time than boys. And our other two friends in our group, Georgia and Lily, were more into horses, so they didn't seem too bothered then that Phia and River got all the attention.

But I was *so* jealous of Phia and River. For so long, I complained to my mum about how no boy ever seemed to want to go out with me. Especially after I'd listen to Phia telling me about the latest guy she'd kissed at whatever party she'd been invited to. It's almost funny—I was desperate then for guys to notice me. I felt like I was missing out, like there was this whole secret club that I wasn't part of. And I just wanted to be 'normal,' even if I wasn't exactly sure what I would do if I had the attention of the guys—because I just didn't understand the sexual attraction that River and Phia were always talking about. But I felt like I had to want it too, want attention from boys and pretend that I was also attracted sexually to them too. I didn't really understand why I didn't want what everyone else seemed to want.

It wasn't until I was at uni that I realized I was on the ace spectrum. Cara had already come out to me a year or so ago about being ace, and when I told her I was probably gray-ace, the two of us had had our own secret 'club.'

"How's the studying going?" I ask Lizzy. She's a year into her part-time history degree with the Open University. She's got this vague idea that when she finishes it she might train to be a teacher, like her mother back in the States, but Lizzy's always going back and forth on what she wants to do once she's finished her studies.

Lizzy gives me a solemn nod. "It's going… Just not very quickly. Anyway, did we catch anything on the wires today?"

"Let me get my laptop." I disappear into my room for a few minutes, grabbing my laptop and a cord. Back in the living room, I hand it all to River. She's the most technologically-gifted out of all of us.

We all eagerly wait as she loads up the audio.

"Okay, this is it," River says, clicking the play button.

I hold my breath and wait.

The sound is muffled. I can't pick out any words.

"We need to do better than this," Lizzy mutters, crestfallen.

"It must be this kit, the quality of it," River says.

"But we can't afford anything better. And we've got to show the world what an unpleasant character this man is," I say.

"Unpleasant character?" Phia laughs. "Now you sound like you're analyzing Charles Dickens."

And that just leads River into doing her best Miss Havisham impression, and, before long, we're all laughing.

NINE

Cara

THE MORNING COMES around all too quickly.

I can't do this.

I can't. I feel sick—it's one of those days. The kind with nausea that makes me dizzy, that makes bright lights drag across my vision. That makes me want to grab onto stuff, anything, to steady myself—even if I know my OCD won't allow it.

I need to cancel. My Lyme disease is flaring, that much is obvious. Sure, it flares with emotional stress, but when I think of all I've done in the last few days—especially going to the club—it's no wonder I'm sicker now. And I was due a flare-up anyway, wasn't I? Plus, if I'm going to push myself, I have to live with the consequences. If I'm going to prove that I'm *not boring*—and, really, I shouldn't have to do that, anyway—I have to pay the price. And, anyway, Lyme's nature is that you get good and bad days. It ebbs and flows. That's part of the reason why it's so hard—almost impossible—for me to plan ahead. This illness isn't reliable.

Why was I thinking last night that a date with Damien wouldn't be so bad? Why did I let my sleep-addled brain persuade me that I could just get it over with? That maybe I would be well enough?

I call Raymond again—I need him to talk me out of backing out—but he doesn't answer. Of course not. He'll be asleep.

Oh, God. Maybe that's a sign that I shouldn't go.

But then I think of the look he'll give me next time we talk, when I tell him I didn't go on the date and…

"You not feeling well?" Mum stares at me across the kitchen counter. "Cara, you look very pale." She reaches behind her for the box of cereal.

"She's nervous about her *date*." Esme practically sings the words, a highly gleeful look on her face.

"Date?" Mum turns back to me in an instant, quick as a flash of lightning. It's a dark day, and the fluorescent strip of the kitchen light reflects off her glasses. "Who with?"

"*Damien Noelle*, of course," Esme says. She says his name like it's a secret that she's letting Mum in on, her eyes all wide and buggy. "Weren't you listening to all her moaning yesterday? *Oh, I wonder if he still likes me* and *I wonder if he still likes true crime*." She makes her voice all low and husky.

"That is a truly horrendous impression of me." I take a few more shaky steps into the kitchen. My knees ache, and my legs feel too weak, soft, insubstantial.

"And now you're going on a date with him?" Mum sounds uncertain.

"I set it up," Esme says gleefully. She digs a spoon into her Rice Krispies with gusto, so much so that milk sloshes over the sides of her bowl.

"Cara, are you well enough for this?" Mum asks. "With the OCD?" She looks doubtful.

I nod, don't trust myself to speak. I grab an apple from the fruit bowl—though, really, we should call it an apple bowl as that's the only type of fruit we ever keep in it. Everything else goes in the fridge—Mum's always worried about fruit spoiling.

I take a bite of the apple and nearly break a tooth. Rock hard. I chew and chew but can't seem to soften my mouthful. When I swallow it, it feels like nails scratching down my throat. My stomach turns.

Lyme makes eating hard. My stomach just feels too heavy most of the time, and then it's hard to swallow. Food just seems to get caught in my throat, like all the words I struggle with.

It'll be over soon, I tell myself. I look ahead—to a few hours' time when I'm back here, when the date's over, when I have showered and washed away every trace of contamination and unease, and can finally relax. I'll watch a film or something in my room as I work on my cartoon—and maybe I won't add Damien the Dashing to it at all, because that would just make it all the more painful. I'll call Raymond and Jana too, after I've done some drawing for a while. And the date with Damien will be long over and I'll feel so much better for it, knowing I can slip back into my current life, however boring it is.

As much as part of me wants Damien to be my boyfriend, to make up for what could've been all those years ago, the OCD has taken over now, and it's trying to protect me. It always does. It knows my room is the safest place to me, and it keeps me there as much as possible, where there's no danger. As much as I hate the OCD, I'm grateful for it as well. I'm more aware now; and I know, also, that that realization is the voice of the OCD, but sometimes it's so difficult to separate it from myself.

"Where are you going?" Mum asks. "On this…date?" She says 'date' like it's a foreign word that she's having difficulty saying.

"Just walking around the park," I say. I thought about it a lot last night, as I tossed and turned, where we would go. I can't handle the woods. There are too many birds there that sit in branches, and too many leaves that could fall on me. The park—even though there could be dogwalkers there—is safer. If I have to choose between bird mess and dogs, I'll pick dogs. Only just though.

"Don't tire yourself out," Mum says. "You've got that blood test later. And appointments next week."

As if I can forget, huh. That's all my life has seemed like for months—blood tests and appointments, preparing for them, processing them afterward whether they've been good or bad, and waiting for the next ones.

Mum makes small talk as I force down the rest of my apple, and Esme tells me disdainfully that I should've tried to make myself look prettier when I'm just about to head out of the door. I look down at my clothes. Wellies, jeans, and a purple hoody. I'm not taking a bag because if a dog jumps up at me, I can stick my clothes in the washing machine afterward, but my bags are all hand wash only. Whenever I've needed to wash them before, I've really struggled. It felt like I could never get them clean enough in the sink, like the water itself was contaminated. I can only really trust the washing machine. So, it is safer not taking a bag. When I'm at the hospital or doctors, I put my things in a disposable carrier bag, but I thought that would look tacky today. On a *date.* A date with Damien—and of course I really like him still.

"You look fine, dear," Mum says, opening the door for me.

"You could put some make up on though," Esme says, giving me a pretty disdainful look for a thirteen-year-old. "I've got that new eyeshadow set. You can borrow it."

"No, thanks." My heart's pounding. Not just because of the makeup I cannot wear because I hate anything touching my face. The only thing I'll tolerate at the moment is sun block, because I have to—the antibiotics I'm on have a warning about severe sunburn as a side effect.

"Be careful," Mum says. "And have a good time."

By the time I near the meeting spot outside High Court Flats, I am most certainly not having a good time. My heart is pounding, my stomach is turning, and twice I stopped on the way here thinking I was going to be sick. Each time, after I'd breathed in crisp air that felt like it was burning me and waited minutes with no vomit appearing, I'd pulled out my phone—careful not to disturb the earphones connected, though I've hardly been able to concentrate on the next chapter of *Luckiest Girl Alive* and will definitely need to re-listen later—ready to text Damien and cancel, but then I couldn't type the message because my hands were shaking too much. I had to pocket my phone safely amid fears that I'd drop it on the road or something. Who knows how many filmy layers of fumes and petrol and dirt would've covered it had I dropped it?

And he's there, outside his building, nonchalantly leaning against the wall. He doesn't care about his clothes touching it. Or his hair—that beautiful silky, blond hair.

Seeing him there makes it hit me—that this is real.

This is a date.

Oh, God. I put my earphones away carefully. I'm on a date. With *Damien.*

I *cannot* do this.

Just as I'm about to turn away, Damien looks up and sees me. And it's too late—I can't turn away now, can't run.

Oh, God.

My legs feel like soggy cardboard as I close the distance between us—careful, though, to keep a foot or two away. Of course.

"Hi," I say, and I read somewhere that when you're with someone who's right for you, it's supposed to feel easy. That when you haven't seen each other for three years, you fall right back into closeness. And I remember what it was like in Mallorca. But already I know that this isn't like that. It can't be.

Too much time has passed. I was a fool to think anything could come of it. This was a bad idea. God. I just need to get today over with. And what, this walk can't last longer than an hour, right?

I mean, if it does, I'll tell him I've got plans later, that I've got to be back home. Yes, I'll do that. I mean, I have got that blood test Mum reminded me of.

"Hi," Damien says, and he leans forward and—

He's going to hug me!

I jump back, my heart pounding. My senses are on high alert, and it's like everything's stopped as I take inventory of the scene—there are three inches between me and Damien, and he didn't touch me. It's okay. It's okay. I jumped backward, but I didn't end up touching anything.

So, it's okay.

"Oh," Damien says. Hurt flashes across his face. "Uh, sorry."

"It's not you..." I say. My words seem too thick all of a sudden. I need to tell him about the Lyme and the OCD—only I can't. Because it just sounds stupid and people don't get it. There are too many misconceptions about OCD, about how it must always be a positive thing, just something that makes you tidy. A neat freak. And fair enough, before I got it, I never realized just how much mental torture is involved in OCD. But I can't tell Damien about it. He might laugh.

I'm ashamed of the OCD too.

I don't want him thinking I'm just making excuses. So, instead, I say nothing more about the near-miss of a hug and swallow hard, desperately wracking my brain for something I can say. I force a smile. Pain flickers down my neck and across my shoulders in the shape of a coat-hanger. "Uh, so, how come you've moved down here?"

"Cheaper rent." His voice sounds strange. He's watching me, but trying to pretend he isn't. I feel my face redden. I've ruined things, I know I have. Of course he's going to think I'm not interested in him now.

I want to scream internally, scream until my voice goes hoarse. Scream until I disappear.

But I don't. I just breathe in the awkward atmosphere. The air's cloggy and makes me feel like I can't breathe fully. Like there's fogginess invading my lungs. Fogginess that's sticky. It makes dark spots hover in front of my eyes.

I pray I won't faint.

"Uh, shall we walk to the park?" I ask.

"Sure," Damien says, and the one-syllable seems so cold and blunt. Not like how he used to be. Not like how *we* used to be.

Oh, God. I really have messed things up.

I need to distract myself, and I need to talk to him—I need to see if we *can* still have that connection we had on the retreat. "Do you still like true crime?"

He seems surprised I remembered, stares at me for a moment. "Yeah, of course."

"What podcasts are you listening to now?" My voice sounds a little forced, and I wince.

"*My Favorite Murder*," he says. "And *Up and Vanished.* They're both good."

"Oh yeah?" I've only listened to a couple episodes of *My Favorite Murder*, but I nod along. I've never been a big podcast listener—I always preferred watching the documentaries and films about true crime or reading crime fiction. There's something thrilling about immersing yourself into these stories, these lives, making your heart beat fast, while having the reassurance that you yourself are safe. "Ah, what's the new series called? I saw it advertised recently? Something like *A Walk in the Dark*?"

"Oh, yeah. *A Walk in the Night*," he says. "I mean, it's mainly about serial killers that do their murders at night. But the episodes so far have been very much focused on sex workers who've been victims, but the speakers seem kind of judgy on the women's work-choices."

"What? Like they're blaming them, not the actual killers?"

Damien nods, wrinkles his nostrils. "Yeah, it's not a good angle to take. Kind of makes me not want to listen to the next episode really. They need to focus more on showing the women as victims, not criticizing them for their work-choice. I mean, the men are the actual murderers here."

"Wow," I say. "I didn't think a podcast would ever take that angle. I thought it had good reviews too."

"It has." He nods. "Because celebrities are backing it. Ah, what's her name?"

I have no idea who he's talking about and shrug.

"Well, I wouldn't recommend it anyway," he says. "They're really judgmental about the victims too, even if they're not sex workers. Like if a victim liked a drink or something, they don't give them the same treatment as other victims who pretty much never touched a drop."

"Like the police with Marnie," I say. "Marnie Wathem? You heard about her? Missing from this town."

"Yes, I heard about that," Damien says as we cross the road. I indicate for us to turn right.

"Heard about it in what way?" I ask. "Because most are saying she's a runaway, but if listening to crime podcasts and reading all those books have taught me anything it's that she probably didn't. Police won't listen though. But just because she was a terror at school, that doesn't mean she can't have been abducted or whatever."

He frowns as he looks at me. "So, you think it is a case?"

I breathe out hard. My breath fogs a little in the air. It's cold for the end of September. "Yeah, I do." Or do I just want it to be? Want that little bit of excitement that it would bring to my life? Especially if I turned out to be right. I've had these whole scenarios constructed in my head of the various different ways I'd prove she was missing and then be the one to save her. In all these scenarios, I'm healthy and well, and I want that to be reality. Even if it does make me selfish. My shoulders squirm. I don't really *want* Marnie to be in danger.

I just want to be better. I want to be strong. I want to do something that makes people notice me for the right reasons. Not write a load of harmful things on my Facebook page.

"Do you know her?" Damien asks.

I shake my head. "Six years younger. I mean, when I was in the sixth form, I think Year 13, she'd just joined the school then? I don't know, but that's as much of a connection as I've got with her. That and us both living in Brackerwood."

He looks disappointed. Maybe he was hoping to ask me more about her—because he's really into true crime, and maybe he wants to play detective too.

Damien the Detective. And maybe I could be his partner, Cara the Crime-Solver.

"Her brother doesn't think she's run away either," Damien says. "I came across his Twitter when I was looking up Marnie's disappearance. He's sure it's a crime."

"Yeah," I say. "He's been putting posters around the town too." I look around, but I can't see. "Not many posters though. Or people keep taking them down." I wouldn't put that past some of the residents of this town—they'll do anything to preserve the idea that Brackerwood is an idyllic place to live. A sleepy little town, taken straight out a film. They don't want to believe that something bad could've happened here.

"I did quite a bit of digging around last night," Damien says a little sheepishly as if he's letting me in on a big secret. "And I agree with the brother. What's his name? Trevor Wathem?" He looks at me questioningly.

I nod.

He starts moving his hands—and I don't know how I could possibly have forgotten just how animated Damien gets when he talks about something he's passionate about. It's really attractive.

"So, Marnie's a big Instagram user," he says. "Trevor talked about that a lot on his Twitter. So, she made no secret on her account that she wanted to be an influencer. And two weeks ago, one of her posts had a comment on from a big-name brand. That seems to be how they contacted her. So, Marnie, started doing these posts about this waterproof makeup or something two days before she disappeared, and she titled them *one of seven* and *two of seven*. And then there was nothing. And it matches up with the dates—the third one should've been on the day she went missing."

A car whizzes past us, churning up exhaust fumes. I try to hold my breath, try to ignore the crawling sensations on my skin.

"So yeah, I looked at that company too—the one that gave her the free makeup, and they repost all their influencers' photos. And they always do like these week-long… I don't know what they're called. Campaigns? So, Marnie didn't finish her work with them. And Trevor was saying too that he was sure that if his sister had run away, she'd still be updating her IG."

I nod. "It does make sense. And what the police are saying about her choosing to run away doesn't match with that—she'd still update the Instagram, surely? Even if she was afraid of her location being tracked, I'm sure she'd find a way. I read that she was going to study computer science at uni too, so she must already know quite a bit. Such as how to hide her location—you know, if she *did* run away." I roll my eyes.

"Computer science?" Damien makes a considering noise in the back of his throat. "Didn't know that."

"Yeah," I say. "I'm not sure where I heard it now." I wrack my brain, but I can't recall it. "But she definitely has skills."

"Do you know Trevor?" Damien asks. "I was thinking maybe I could contact him, say that I want to help look for her. Or would that look suspicious?"

I raise my eyebrows. "A complete stranger? I think that could look a bit suspicious."

"You don't know him then?"

I shake my head. "Not well enough for that. I mean, until Marnie disappeared I didn't even know he existed. Apparently there are other siblings as well. I think someone said that some of them are adopted, but I'm not sure which ones. But that's about all I know of the Wathem family."

Damien looks disappointed. "Do you know any of her friends?"

"I don't think so."

I try desperately to think of something else to say, but I can't. It's like my thought processes have suddenly become shut off. A huge great boulder has come down in my brain, flattened everything else that was there. I groan and know that I'm close to using up all my energy now.

We reach the park and walk around the perimeter. As we walk, my coat-hanger pain gets stronger, and then my left hip is hurting too—it does this, on and off. A flare-up of the joint last for days. My NHS GP could never explain that pain, but my private doctor, Dr. Singh the Savior was able to account for it after a quick lot of tests.

"Joint pain is common in chronic Lyme," he'd said. "Particularly the big, major joints. Knees, shoulders, hips.

Lyme arthritis—the bacteria gets inside the joints, invades them. You get swelling in the joints, a lot of pain, because the lining of the joints is being eaten away by the bacteria."

Bacteria from the Lyme that the NHS doctors swore I couldn't possibly have anymore because they don't believe that chronic Lyme disease exists. Ha. To them, I'm just a hypochondriac.

Damien and I make small talk—not about Marnie now. Or rather, he makes small talk and I try to keep up—but my head's feeling too heavy, and my thoughts are slow now. I stare at Damien's hand as we walk. How it hangs freely at his side. My hand's in my hoody pocket, so it can't accidentally brush against his.

Damien asks a few questions about other places to walk around here. And I feel like I can't even think now. The fogginess that was in my lungs has now reached my brain. My mind's too heavy. It's like I'm swimming through sticky tar as I try to arrange my thoughts, work out something coherent and cool that I can say.

"Yeah, there are some cool walks." And I do know this. I used to run cross country all around here.

Oh, God. I sound stupid. Absolutely stupid. And uninterested in him—he's going to wonder why I even came on this date. I sigh, trying to channel back the energy I had only a few minutes ago, when we were discussing Marnie. But I can't. I'm too tired now. The fatigue is crushing over me.

It's strange how it happens—how quickly I change. How quickly Lyme changes a person, even on a minute-by-minute basis. Because one minute I can be animated and appear not sick at all, but then the exhaustion gets me and everything's a struggle. And I don't want Damien seeing me like this—I'm not the fun girl he met before.

I'm a shadow of my former self, and walking with him, struggling to keep up with him and the forced conversation just makes me angry now. My Lyme is winning yet again, just reminding me that I can't ever have *normal.*

I'm relieved when an hour's passed. When I can make an excuse to Damien about why I've got to leave. When I know I can finally get home and rest. I know I should feel proud for actually managing to do this, but all I feel like is a failure. My hip feels like it's on fire, and my neck and shoulders feel too tight. My vision's blurring and a couple times I'm sure I've sounded drunk.

Damien seems surprised, but doesn't try to stop me. He's probably finding this as awkward as I am now. Probably wondering why I asked for this date at all.

I say a quick goodbye, ready to duck out of the way of another hug—but he doesn't even attempt it. Just nods. And that's it.

Tears fill my eyes as I walk home. He's not going to contact me again. Why would he? I really am Cara the Calamity—and sure, it's a bit over-the-top, but I can never think of many words beginning with C that aren't Crazy or Catastrophe.

TEN

Cara

TEARS BLIND ME as I stare at my graphics tablet. I've been trying to work on a sketch of Riley for several hours, trying to calm myself ever since I returned from that disastrous date, before I have to leave for the blood test. I've been meaning to add Riley into the cartoon for a while now, but I just can't stop thinking about the date, recalling it all in excruciating detail.

It was going great when we were talking about Marnie, even if I'd avoided the hug, and then I'd messed it all up. All because of this stupid illness.

It's completely stolen my life. Sometimes, I feel like I'm just a ghost. I'm so different to how I was before, and I hate it. I'm not *me* anymore.

I think one of the worst things about it is that, in the UK at least, it's a controversial diagnosis. Chronic Lyme disease isn't recognized by the NHS. It's almost like it's not supposed to exist. Whenever I go to my doctor with all my symptoms she always says it can't possibly be the Lyme disease still.

"You had the treatment for it," she says. "Three weeks of antibiotics would've been enough to clear it."

But it wasn't.

Okay, so at the time I believed it was—because you believe doctors automatically, right? You believe them, no question about it. Until you have reason not to.

Three years ago, only a few months after the retreat, I was on a camping holiday with Jana, River, Phia, and Lizzy, and I'd been bitten by a tick. Lizzy had completely freaked out and gone into Google-all-about-Ticks mode and insisted I go to the emergency department. There, the doctors thought I was overacting, I was sure. One of them even said I could've pulled the tick out myself with tweezers, but Lizzy kept asking if I was going to get antibiotics. They'd sort of humored me and my group—five giddy young women in their early twenties, panicking about nothing and believing everything they'd read online. At last, they did agree to give me a three-week course of antibiotics, but kept emphasizing that it was a precaution and mainly because the head of the tick had got stuck and they'd had to spend twenty excruciating minutes gouging it out with sterilized needles and tweezers.

"Lyme disease is very rare," they'd said. "But this will make sure you don't get it."

I popped each of the required pills, exactly on time, for the next three weeks. And I felt fine. Yay, I'd avoided Lyme disease!

It wasn't until a month or so later after I had finished the antibiotics that I began to feel *very* unwell. The fatigue was the first thing. It was like a bucket of tiredness had been poured over me, a never-ending bucket, and I could never get away from the torrent of it. My joints began to ache. My muscles would protest at the slightest thing. Then came the heart problems. Just getting out of bed became difficult because my heart rate would soar, getting higher and higher until my blood pressure plummeted, leaving me in a collapsed mess on the floor as I grappled with unconsciousness.

The GP said it was anxiety, at that point. I mean, Mum even asked about the possibility of Lyme, but she was shot down quick as lightning. I'd been treated for Lyme. This was just anxiety. Nothing to worry about. Huh.

My symptoms escalated from there. Within a few months, I was fainting multiple times a day. My chest constantly felt heavy. It was a struggle to breathe after walking upstairs. Eventually, the NHS doctors diagnosed me with Postural Orthostatic Tachycardia Syndrome. They said it was common in teenage girls and young women. I was 22 then. And they presented it to me like it was the answer to all my troubles.

But POTS is just a collection of symptoms, all the websites say that. It's a syndrome. It has a cause. And when all the drugs the doctors and consultants were giving me didn't help, I began doing research trying to find out what caused this condition. Lyme disease came up time and time again in this research. No surprise there.

"But you were successfully treated for Lyme disease," my GP said, rolling her eyes, when I brought up my research, maybe for the second or third time. She was clearly sick of me taking up time in her office now, and always asking the same questions. "Three weeks would've gotten rid of it definitely. It can't be Lyme disease. It really is just POTS."

"So why didn't the Fludrocortisone and Midodrine help the POTS?"

She didn't have an answer.

I was passed from doctor to doctor under the NHS as they tried to work out why my POTS wasn't responding to the usual drugs. Other conditions were ruled out, but still I was getting worse, sicker and sicker as my life was sucked away.

Eventually, I struggled walking *anywhere*, not just upstairs. I told my Mum I thought I was dying. How could I be this sick and doctors not diagnose me with anything? The medical professionals began to blame anxiety again—something I'd read was likely to happen.

Six months passed, and I was a prisoner inside my useless body. My friends began to disappear, all apart from Jana. Even though I couldn't meet up with them all, she'd still make an effort to call me. But I heard the others talking, once. Lizzy the Levelheaded and River the Repulsive and Phia the Flawless.

"If there was something actually wrong with her, doctors would've found it by now," River had said once. "They know what they're doing."

"But those articles said chronic Lyme is a thing," Lizzy had replied.

"But it's not chronic Lyme, is it?" River snorted. "Cara told us her GP said it isn't. So, it isn't. She's just wanting it to be. But this is all in her head."

My heart had sunk. My own 'friends' thought I was crazy. It didn't take long for the doctors to agree with my so-called friends. And I suppose when, a year later, I started hallucinating and developed severe OCD overnight it didn't help my case.

And I was now scared of everything.

I hated the psychiatrist I was assigned. All he wanted to do was pump me full of antidepressants and antipsychotics. He said it was all a mental health problem, just like River had said. The psychiatrist said it was a reaction to trauma—though what trauma he thought I'd endured, I still don't know. Countless hours were wasted in his office. He said I just needed to try a bit harder to overcome the OCD.

Nothing helped. Not antidepressants, not antipsychotics, not the rounds of talk therapy.

My right side was seizing up. Doctors said it was a manifestation of anxiety. Mum argued with them.

"How can this be anxiety?" she'd asked, pointing at the doctor. Her nails had been bitten right down that day, I remember. "Look, it doesn't make sense! Cara used to be on the cross-country team at school, and at uni she played Netball. She was active, sporty—now she's struggling to move."

Under protest, the NHS arranged for a neurologist to see me. He noted weakness on my right side, and I thought that was the moment where these doctors would finally start taking me seriously. But then he said it wasn't something he would look into because he supported the mental health diagnosis I had been given.

"No one believes me, Mum," I said one day.

"I do," she said. "Your dad does. Esme does. The people who matter believe you." But at that point, I wasn't sure it was enough. I needed *doctors* to believe me.

I was constantly nauseated, my handwriting had changed, my hair was falling out leaving huge bald patches on the side of my crown. I was in so much pain. My hallucinations of cats wouldn't leave me alone. I was terrified of everything.

I was depressed—how could I not be? I wasn't myself anymore—I couldn't do my sports, had had to abandon my goal of being an illustrator, and couldn't even play with my dog. My life had fallen down a sinkhole, and I was miserable. Of course this 'confirmed' the doctors' diagnosis that this was a mental health problem. Even though the depression and OCD were symptoms, not a cause. I was sinking in a sea of despair. When I reported new symptoms to the doctors—physical symptoms, because by then I'd made sure not to tell them how I was feeling mentally—they humored me with little laughs. No new referrals were made, because I was just a crazy girl.

Dad had been doing research for months, and he'd printed out more and more scientific journal articles about how Lyme causes encephalitis—brain inflammation—as evidence for me to take to appointments.

"This causes the neuropsychiatric symptoms," I said. And maybe it was a bad idea, taking evidence in like that. No doctor likes to be proven wrong.

The NHS would not test for encephalitis, even when I brought it up with different doctors at the GP practice. Even when I phoned the neurologist's receptionist. Instead, it was all reported back to my psychiatrist as 'further evidence' that I 'wanted' to be ill.

"But this is what I have!" I felt like shouting as I waved Dad's research.

But the NHS didn't want me to have it. They didn't want me to get better, that's how it felt.

Mum and Dad sold their shares of the business they ran with my aunt and uncle—my aunt and uncle who no longer let me see my cousins for fear they'd 'catch' my madness—and my parents got some money. We went privately with Dr. Singh, a doctor who said he could diagnose encephalitis caused by chronic Lyme disease, and arrange for the tests to prove I had chronic Lyme—and, crucially, he could treat it too.

I took long trips to London by train, where I went to private clinics and had my blood drawn for expensive lab tests that would be done in Germany and the US.

The Cunningham panel sent to Oklahoma detected high levels of auto-antibodies attacking the receptors in my brain, specifically the Basal ganglia. Proof of encephalitis. The private doctor told me this is commonly caused by Lyme disease and that my Armin lab results, the ones from Germany, showed my body was fighting an active Lyme infection.

It was amazing that moment knowing that I wasn't really crazy, not that there's anything wrong with being crazy, but knowing that there was a doctor on my side and that I could get better was wonderful. It's a long process, years and years. And I'm right at the start of the treatment now. Only a couple months in.

ELEVEN

Damien

"DAMIEN!" CARA'S EYES light up as she sees me in the games room. She's smiling as she makes her way toward where I'm sitting. And wow, I like the way she says my name. My name sounds like velvet or something on her lips.

I was waiting for the guys—another session of table tennis is planned—but seeing Cara here, suddenly I know I couldn't care less about the next day of The Ace Table Tennis League. Especially when David's going to be there; I heard him bad-mouthing me and Cara, saying that we cheated on that challenge this morning. He was clearly just jealous that we got the chocolate.

No, I want to talk to Cara now, get to know her, because she's fascinating.

Earlier today, as we enjoyed the chocolate we'd won—much to the incredulous looks of all those around us—we'd talked. She studied illustration, and she's a wicked artist too. Amazing at doing caricatures. She drew a quick one of Mrs. Mitchell, had her leaping out of a jack-in-the box from behind a tree, and she even let me keep it.

"It's just a quick sketch," she'd said, and her eyes were modest, and that just made me like her even more.

"How are you?" I ask her now, and I scoot over, make room for her on the wide armchair.

"Good," she says with the most adorable smile as she sits next to me. "You?" Her voice is chirpy—almost as chirpy as Jana's. But whereas with Jana that chirpiness makes her seem like an overexcited puppy, it almost makes Cara seem more... I don't know, sincere. Like she really wants to know how I am.

"I'm good too," I say.

Her leg brushes against mine as she pushes her hair back over her shoulder. It's slightly damp, like she just stepped out the shower not long ago. I can smell her shampoo. Citrus.

"I hope we're paired up again tomorrow," she says.

Me too. I nod. Oh, God, if we're not it's going to be torture. "Is there another challenge tomorrow?"

Cara nods quickly. Her eyes are bright. "There's one each day. Anyway, what are you doing in here?"

"I was waiting for the guys... Don't know if they're actually going to show."

"That's like a line in the podcast I was just listening to," Cara says. "'How were the girls to know that killers were going to show?'" She imitates a man's deep voice, and then blushes. "Sorry, I don't know why I just did that."

But I'm staring at her, my heart pounding, because I know that podcast. "What Happened to Elizabetta Jackson?" *I lean in closer. "You listen to that podcast too?"*

Her eyes widen. "Oh my God! You know it?"

"Avid listener," I say.

Elizabetta Jackson disappeared from a sleepy US town thirty years ago. What Happened to Elizabetta Jackson *is a new podcast from some college students majoring in journalism who promised to uncover the truth about the missing fourteen-year-old.*

"No way!" Cara's eyes are bright. "I can't wait to listen to the next episode," she says. "I'm sure it was the cousin, Levi. Did you hear how suspicious he sounded in that interview?"

I nod. "Right! I mean, he kept changing his story—and I know the presenter is really going to grill him for that next time. I can't believe it's a monthly podcast though. So long to wait!"

She leans in closer to me still. "It's just a great podcast—I mean, a lot of true crime ones are, but this one just has so many layers. Like, it's just amazing."

"I know. I mean, when I first started listening to podcasts I had this idea that I'd run my own one in the future. A stupid idea, but then listening to this new one just made me more determined."

"It would be amazing to make your own," Cara agrees, and her voice is kind of breathy. "And I'd definitely listen to it. You have a lovely voice."

A lovely voice? I feel myself blush. I nod and try to think of something else to say, but I can't. My head's just gone blank.

"Anyway, you want to play a game?" Cara asks, smiling. She turns her head, and I see she's got a light layer of lip gloss on when it catches the light.

A stack of board games leans precariously to the right, in front of us, and she leans forward, tilting her head to one side as she reads the names.

We pick one at random, then pull over a low-standing coffee table. Cara moves to sit on the floor on the other side of it, and the moment she's gone, my leg feels cold without her body heat against it.

"Bet I'll beat you." She gives me the cutest little smile.

"Oh, we'll see about that," I say.

TWELVE

Damien

CARA COULDN'T HAVE made it clearer if she'd tried—the message was loud and clear. She isn't interested in me. She didn't even want me touching her. She'd looked positively terrified of me—her face so pale and her eyes so wide and frightened. And it was just a friendly hug—nothing more. My stomach tightens. I don't understand. I'd thought her text had sounded flirtatious. Thought she'd been thinking about me as much as I'd been thinking about her all these years. Of course she hasn't. Because no one else gets caught up on someone the way I apparently do.

I stare at my phone screen. For the last few hours I've been trying to work out if I should text her. Say I'm sorry. Because I should apologize right? I mean, we had had a good conversation at first, but then it was like she'd drifted off somewhere else. Like she kept having to remind herself that she was supposed to be talking to me. Like it was a huge effort on her part.

The rest of that walk had been so awkward. It was strange—awkward was one thing I'd never guessed it would be. Not given how well the two of us had got on in Mallorca. There, we'd just clicked almost instantly. It had given me hope that even though I'm ace, I could find someone that I'd work with romantically, someone who wouldn't want the slightest touch to lead to sex all the time.

Because that's the experience I'd had before. My last—and only—relationship. I was twenty-one, and I'd got involved with this woman I thought was amazing. Things were great—we clicked and hit it off. I wanted to spend all my time with her—until she was no longer satisfied with just kissing or just cuddling.

Until everything became about sex—or rather, about why we weren't doing it as often as she wanted.

"What are you? Gay?" she'd screamed at me once. "You're supposed to want me! You're a man! Be a man!"

"That's not fair," I'd shouted back. "You know about my sexuality—"

"You said you were demisexual!" She had tears in her eyes. "You said you'd be sexually attracted to me once we'd formed a close connection, and we have, haven't we?"

"Yes, but—"

"So why aren't we doing it all the time then? Seriously, it's been months, Damien. *Months.* Is it me? Is it just that you don't want to sleep with me? Is it me? Am I repulsive?" Her eyes widened. "Is there someone else?"

"No!"

"Then it has to be me. You're not attracted to *me*."

"I am! I am," I'd cried. "It's just…"

It was just sometimes I *did* want to have sex, really felt that attraction, and I was sexually attracted to her—the only person

I'd been attracted to like that. And we did have sex, those times, and when we did it was amazing. But most of the time, I *didn't* feel like that. I didn't feel that attraction. Maybe 'demisexual' was the wrong label for me to use, because doesn't that mean you're going to want to sleep with your partner all the time? Or have I got that wrong? I'm still not sure, and I've never really been brave enough to talk about it to other people. I just find aceness confusing, even—especially my own aceness.

I'd signed up for the ace retreat a few months after she and I had broken up, thought that I'd learn proper definitions there and be able to say with certainty what I was. I thought there'd be games where we'd have to match up the label with the definition. But Mrs. Mitchell never really talked about definitions. The whole time was more about getting to know each other as people, not labels. And, as Mrs. Mitchell said at several points, labels can change and you can change which ones you identify with. There's no right or wrong way to identify. I just wish I actually understood what it meant for me.

In the late afternoon, I head out to the library. It's the next place on my list for where I can put up my business cards. So far, I've only got a weekly walk with Mrs. East's dog, Rufus, and if I'm going to keep up with my rent payments to Cody, I need to find more work. Maybe I should look at doing something other than dog-walking too. Maybe it's naive to think I can make enough from that alone.

The library's on the corner of the main street, and it's empty except for a group of women in their mid-twenties.

My eyes widen. I recognize the woman with the black hair.

"Jana?" I say. She turns, and it is her. I look at the other women quickly. One of them is white, one is Black, and one is Asian. Cara isn't among them. I breathe a sigh of relief.

Jana sweeps her dark eyes over me. "Sorry? Who are you?"

"Uh, Damien." My voice croaks a little. She looks good. Her makeup is subtle, and I find myself appreciating the curves of her body. "From Mallorca." I purposefully don't call it the 'ace retreat' because I don't want to out myself to Jana's friends, and I don't know if Jana is out to them either.

Jana does a double take. "Oh, wow! Hi." She quickly does introductions. The Asian woman is called Phia, and the Black woman is Lizzy. River is the other white woman. We all exchange pleasantries, and then the others say they have to get going—apparently they're on a quick break from work, leaving their boss to man the fort—and all of a sudden it's just me and Jana here.

"Does Cara know you're here?" Jana asks.

"I bumped into her, yeah," I say. And I want to say we went on a date this morning—only it was clearly not a date, in her eyes.

"You two were like two peas in a pod," Jana says, wistfully.

"I suppose." I swallow hard. "But nothing happened. I spoke to her this morning actually, and I just didn't feel it anymore. Was just… It was like we were different people."

Jana nods. "Yeah, that can happen. Anyway, what are you doing?"

I explain my new living situation and how I'm looking for work.

Jana's eyes widen. "You're not a waiter, are you?"

"Dog-walker."

"So, you couldn't *be* a waiter?" There's a strange intonation in her tone. "It's my boss—at *The Red Panda*, just across the road. He's being a right sexist pig. And racist. He's only employed women so far, but I wonder if you just went up to him, asked if he had any work, if he'd give you any? Please, you'd be doing us a huge favor."

"Uh, okay… Right."

"You'll do it?" Jana's eyes flash with gratitude. "No harm in trying, right? Come on. He doesn't close for another half hour."

Before I can say another word, she's leading me out of the library and across the road to a tiny café that's set back from the main street. *The Red Panda*, the sign reads, along with a cartoon of a cheeky-looking red panda. Inside, I can see Lizzy and Phia in there now, both tying aprons on and not looking very happy. A balding man, excruciatingly tall, is watching them.

"Go on," Jana says, giving me a little prod.

Everything's happening at once, way too fast like the reel of time has been sped up, and then the bell's chiming as I open the door. Its hinges creak.

The man—Mr. Richards, Jana told me—turns to me, his eyes like a hawk.

"About to close! Can't you read?" he snaps.

Wow. What a way to talk to people who could be customers! And there's clearly still half an hour to go according to the sign on the door.

"Sorry," I say. "I was just going to ask if there's any work going?"

Lizzy and Phia have both stopped and are staring at me.

Mr. Richards's eyes narrow until he can't possibly see me. "Not hiring," he snaps. "Get out."

I get out. Jana's waiting to the side a few feet away, out of sight of the windows of the café.

"Well?" she asks.

I shake my head. "Sorry. He practically bit my head off."

She looks wistful. "It was worth a try."

"Yeah," I say. My voice trailing. There's a spark in her eyes that's brimming with energy. "Uh, do you want to get a drink? Like now?" I ask. And jeez, what is it about me? Going from one girl to another? Finding myself a date straight away because Cara rejected me?

Jana raises her eyebrows for a second and looks at me—the kind of look I can tell where she really drinks me in. She smiles slowly. "Sure. But anywhere but the one with the racist, sexist boss."

"Of course," I say. "I mean, they're not serving new customers now, anyway." I laugh.

"There's a great place on West Street. Stays open late too. I'll show you."

THIRTEEN

Cara

"A SMALL SCRATCH," the NHS nurse says, but she looks gleeful as she stabs me with the needle. Of course it's more than just a small scratch—it always is—and I blink quickly, trying to stop my eyes from smarting.

I have to have my thyroid and liver checked monthly while I'm on the private treatment for Lyme, and my consultant, Dr. Singh, wrote to my GP to ask if this could be done on the NHS. I'd fully expected a point-blank refusal, but surprisingly, they agreed to do the blood draws, rather than demand I went to the private doctor who was requesting it for this. That had shocked me, and I wonder still whether it's a half-admission from my GP that she thinks something is going on but knows that the NHS system isn't able to treat it, constrained by guidelines.

The nurse tries to make small talk as she siphons my blood away, and I try to follow whatever it is she's saying—really boring stuff anyway—as I stare at the ceiling. My vision wobbles and immediately anxiety jumps into my throat. Is that my vision going because I'm starting to lose consciousness?

I've never fainted before during a blood test, but ever since I began fainting at random times, I've been convinced that the sight of blood is going to set me off. So that's why I stare at the ceiling, tense and on edge. I used to lie down on the couch when my blood was being taken, but I can't now. Can't let my hair touch it. The upright chair is safer—even if it does mean I may be more likely to faint. And then what would happen? Would I slump back into the chair and contaminate my hair against its leather surface anyway? Would I fall on the floor, spelling out even more disaster?

I need to distract myself. I try to think of the latest events in the book I'm reading—what's currently happening to Ani, the main character in *Luckiest Girl Alive*. And she's such a great character, so dark and twisty, one of my favorites, but my brain's all foggy now and I can't remember anything that happened in the last chapter I listened to.

"All done," the nurse says, her voice that fake kind of cheery that you speak to young children with. As if I'm definitely not an adult.

I scurry out of the room as fast as I can. Mum's in the waiting room.

"Everything all right?" she asks. "You've gone very pale."

"I'm fine."

"Guess it was that walk this morning," she says.

"I guess." My voice is dull, like it's not really there and my words are floating away.

"It's a shame that didn't go well," she says, because that's what I told her, focusing solely on the second half of the walk and not the first half where I actually felt we had a connection. Before I ran out of energy and ruined it.

I take a deep breath. Have I really ruined it? What if I can re-harness some of that energy first? Damien and I originally bonded over our love of crime—it was talking about crime on the retreat that really connected us. And we still had that connection today, when talking about Marnie.

Maybe, just maybe, if I can talk to him more about it, make him see that we still have that connection, then things could start to work again? And when things are working, then I could tell him about the Lyme? Make him understand why I'm most likely giving out mixed signals.

And if we were investigating Marnie's case together, that would be a great way for us to bond. And even save Marnie too?

I look around. Mum's now at the counter—she wants to leave a message for Esme's doctor about her ears. Before I can chicken out, I grab my phone and text Damien, right from the reception of the medical center.

I've been thinking a lot about what you said about Marnie, and I agree, we should look into it more. Maybe I can find someone who knows her?

I click send before I can change my mind. I drum my fingers on my thigh as I wait for a response.

Then I realize what Mum said.

A shame? She'd rather I had a boyfriend?

Then again, she probably would rather she had a normal daughter. One who isn't afraid of everything.

"We've just got to pick up your prescription," Mum says as she returns. We head outside. "Then we can get back home. But we'll drive to Boots."

I'm relieved we're driving there. I feel shaky and weak and my OCD's getting worse. Even the air seems dangerous.

Although I don't like sitting in cars, I'd rather be in there right now. The air is probably safer in there.

My head's spinning with thoughts of safety and danger as we get into the car, and my OCD's telling me how I'll need to shower when I'm home—going through the process in excruciating detail as it tells me the order I need to take my clothes off in to avoid contaminating myself further.

Mum hums under her breath as she starts the car. The engine sounds throaty. I don't like loud sounds now. They grate right through me. I'm tense, on edge, as she drives, and we weave our way down the main street of the town.

Mum turns left onto West Street, where Boots, the pharmacy, is. There's one free car parking space on the side of the road and Mum coaxes her old Ford into it.

"You staying here?" she asks.

I nod. I feel too weak to get out. I check my phone. Damien's not replied.

"I won't be long, but I'll pop in at the green-grocers too. Esme needs some strawberries for her food tech lesson tomorrow."

I nod. My heart's pounding, and I feel sick. I look at my coat sleeve as Mum gets out and walks away. Every time I have a blood test done and they put their wad of cotton wool over the site, taping it down with white opaque tape that reminds me of masking tape, I half expect my blood to soak through. That one day I'll bleed endlessly and endlessly, and lines of red will show through my sleeve.

But it doesn't happen.

Good. I can't imagine how my OCD would react if it did.

I breathe out a deep breath and look out of the window and—

It's Damien and Jana, sitting inside a café window, less than ten feet from me. The panes of glass separate us.

I feel like I've been punched in the gut as I watch Jana laughing at something Damien's said. Watch as Jana lightly places her hand on Damien's arm. Watch as he looks up into her face and smiles.

Oh, God. I lean back in my seat, turning my head away so I can't see them—and so they can't see me if they look up.

My best friend and Damien—they're on a *date*.

FOURTEEN

Cara

SOMETIMES I WONDER what it would've been like, if I'd just been Cara the Confident and called Damien three years ago. If I'd overcome my shyness and just picked up the damn phone, not leaving it two weeks before deciding to make a move, by which point I discovered I'd lost the book he'd written his number in. Maybe we'd have gone out several times, and maybe when the girls invited me on that camping holiday I'd have refused because Damien and I would've had plans. Maybe he'd have taken me on a romantic holiday or something. Paris or Rome. Maybe we'd have been eating dinner at a posh restaurant, so I'd never have been at the campsite. I'd never have been bitten by the tick. I'd never have caught Lyme disease. I'd never have developed encephalitis. My brain would be normal. Not inflamed. I wouldn't have OCD. I'd be able to lie in Damien's arms without a constant spiel in my head, without thinking about how to safely decontaminate myself, without feeling possessed by thoughts I know are irrational, but I have no control over.

Maybe. Maybe. Maybe.

Tears burn the corners of my eyes, and I'm angry. Angry at the life I could've had. How happy I could've been. The suffering I could've avoided.

I take a deep breath. No. I can't think like that. All it does is upset me. I know that. I dream often enough about what my life could've been like.

Mum gets back into the car, and I'm trying not to cry, trying not to show her that there's anything wrong.

It's my own fault, I tell myself. I made Damien think I wasn't interested.

But Jana… my best friend?

I swallow a gulp as silently as I can, grateful when Mum starts the drive home.

I shower meticulously, going through all my rituals four times—once more than usual—before I turn the hot water off. I dry myself with my towel, careful to dry myself in the correct order, and then deposit the towel into the laundry basket. I have to use a fresh one for each shower. Can't reuse, because I can almost see all the dead skin cells on a once-used towel. All the contamination. All the badness. Can't get that all on my body again. I've only just got it off.

Mum leaves to go and pick Esme up from school, and the house is eerily silent. I'd planned to watch a film or draw or something, but I can't bring myself to do it. I just lie on my bed. My head spins and spins and I feel sick. My joints are aching a lot too, and I'm just so tired. Too tired to even listen to more of my book. I just stare with bleary eyes at my bookcase—all my favorite crime novels are up there: *Sharp Objects* by Gillian Flynn, *The Other Woman* by Sandie Jones, *The Wife Between Us* by Greer Hendricks, and *Before I Go to Sleep* by S.J. Watson. Those have prime position on my shelf. Paperbacks and hardcovers that I now struggle to read. Listening to audio is much easier with Lyme now.

I blink, groggily. The books seem to move, dancing a little. I shake my head.

Sleep. I need to sleep.

But I dream of Damien, of course I do. I dream that we're together, and I haven't got OCD or Lyme, and that he's not going on dates with Jana, and when I wake up, I am crying.

There's tinkering sounds downstairs along with Esme's voice. And another one. Esme's friend.

My phone rings. It's Jana.

I don't want to answer it. Revulsion pulls through me. Jana and Damien. I feel sicker.

She's my best friend. I let her leave a message. She doesn't.

An hour later, Damien replies to my text.

Sure! Sounds great. I can't do tomorrow but can meet the day after?

I stare at the message for a long, long time. Does that mean he's not with Jana? I mean, it's only been one date…and there could be a chance they were just meeting as friends. It might not even have been a date.

Have I still got a chance?

FIFTEEN

Jana

"HEY, GIRL." I wedge my phone between my shoulder and ear, cradling it there like everyone on TV seems to do and—

My phone slips, because of course it does, and whatever answer's Cara's giving, well, only the carpet hears it.

"Shoot," I mutter. I flap my hands about, my nails are still wet, and try to turn my phone over with one hand, hoping I can use the ace ring on my finger as some sort of lever—not that it works. Typical—I've been trying to get through to Cara since yesterday evening, and now that she finally answers, more than twelve hours later, I've got wet nails.

"River!" I flick my head back toward the doorway. Is River still in the apartment? She was the one who called Cara's number for me and slid my phone into the gap between my neck and shoulder, helping me with the practicalities of making a phone call when one's hands are otherwise engaged. And that was only seconds ago, really. Cara answered on the eighth ring.

But there's no sound now. Did my roommate leave already? In the time it took Cara to answer her phone? I can hear Cara's voice muffled against the carpet.

"Hold on, Car," I say loudly. Maybe I can put it onto speakerphone without smudging crimson across the screen or messing up my nails.

Eventually, I manage it. But the whole thing has me wheezing. Need to use my inhaler. Damn asthma.

"Are you okay?" Cara's voice is a bit alarmed now. No wonder, what with my shouting. I wonder if the line made a weird noise when I dropped the phone too.

"Yeah, just painted my nails, trying not to smudge them, but dropped my phone." I clear my throat. "Anyway, girl, I wanted to ask you something. Well, check with you on something." My voice is going all crackly. I sound nervous.

"Yeah?"

"So, you'll never guess who I bumped into yesterday—Damien! From the retreat."

I wait for her reaction—surprise and exclamations. But there's nothing, just Cara's quick breaths.

"Anyway, we got talking, and I asked him if he'd want to meet again, with me—and then I felt like such a terrible friend. Like I'm creeping behind your back or something, so I just wanted to ask you if you're okay with it? Like, if I do go out with him?"

I swallow quickly, the air seems too hot in here. I glance at my nails. There are tiny hairs from the carpet sticking to them. Great.

"That's fine," Cara says. Her voice is neutral. There's no emotion in it.

"Are you sure?" I frown. "Because I know you liked him—"

"That was three years ago, Jana. It's fine, honest."

River cannot stop laughing when I tell her that I'm going out with Damien because she also listened to Cara mope after him for months. The two of us are heading into town later that day, once I've done my shift at the café, to do the weekly shop at Waitrose. It's the most expensive shop in town, but River says it's much better quality and seeing how she pays for food for both of us—because I pay the water and internet bills—I let it slide.

"I bet she's secretly crying now," River says.

"Hey, don't be mean," I say. "And she won't be." Cara had said it was fine with her—and I believe her. Don't I? I mean, it was three years ago. And she never actually called Damien. Just told me she didn't want to, in the end.

"*Of course* she's going to be crying now." River laughs as she grabs a clementine, then brings it close to her face to inspect it for imperfections. "I mean, what else has she got to do? She doesn't even work."

"She's ill, Riv," I say, giving her a look.

"Is she, though?"

"She told us what her new doctor said."

"Yeah, but that's a *private* doctor. Pay them enough, and they'll say whatever you want." She tosses the clementine into the trolley, apparently not caring that it'll bruise or whatever thanks to that movement, even after inspecting it so carefully.

I give her a look. "That's not how it works. You can't fake blood test results, anyway. And you can see how ill she is now."

River makes a noncommittal sound. "I'm just saying, that's all. And, really, she does need to just pull herself together like her shrink said."

As River rambles on and on, I think how it's no wonder that Cara doesn't come to our Tuesday Girls' Nights anymore. Sometimes, I just want to grab River by the shoulders and shake her hard. I mean, I've tackled her about it before—but River's just one of those people who doesn't believe that any illness can be chronic. Half the time, I almost want her to get struck down by Lyme too—maybe then she'd have some sympathy for Cara. But then that's me being a bad person, wishing Cara's struggles on another.

"Oh, watch out." River's eyes focus on something—or someone—behind me. "Incoming."

I turn and see—

Oh, God.

Max. My ex.

He's a scruffy guy, always has been and always will be. At least now he's not shoving his tongue down my cousin's throat. Anastacia's nowhere in sight. Thank God.

"Jana!" Max holds his arms out in a wide hugging motion.

"No." I hold my hands up in the universal stop sign. "I mean it, Max. *No.*"

He glances at River, then steps closer to me. "Please, Jana. I just want to talk."

"I don't want to talk to you."

"But we were good together!" His voice is close to a whine. "We were—you can't deny it."

"We were good together?" I snort. "You actually believe that? You lied to me, Max."

River's eyes widen—they always do when she's witnessing drama. I try to ignore her.

"Lied?" Max frowns.

"Saying you were okay with me being ace."

"You did say you were *gray-ace*."

"Gray-ace is still part of the asexual spectrum." I lower my voice. "And you know I'm closer to the ace end than not."

"Look, we can work something out," he says, pleadingly. "It's all about compromise. And I know you love sex really. It's just a phase you're going through, pretending to be…." *Ace*, he mouths the word.

"A phase?" I stare at him. "Really? Is that what you're going with?"

"Jana, please. Is it just because of that time when—"

"It's because I'm asexual and you're not respectful at all of my sexuality." I glare at him, then realize quite a few shoppers are staring at us, apparently enjoying the show as much as River is. "We're not getting back together," I say. "End of."

Max's eyes darken.

I exhale loudly, daring him to say another word. He doesn't.

River watches him leave, a second clementine in her hand. "Girl, he's not gonna give up easy, you know."

SIXTEEN

Cara

"OH, CARA," RAYMOND the Reassurer says.

"It's fine. It's fine." I try to keep the emotion out of my voice, but he's my friend and I know it's futile hiding from him how upset I really am that Jana's going on another date with Damien. My Damien—except he's not mine. I know that. He's not interested in me—not like that anyway. And I probably made him think that I only wanted to be friends. It's my fault.

"Do you want to talk about it?" Raymond asks.

I shake my head. "Definitely not." I take a deep breath. My eyes blur for a second, my vision separating into two different fields, left eye and right eye. Double vision. I blink, feel nausea working its way upward. I swallow quickly and flex my fingers, make fists. Concentrate on my hands. "How'd your appointment go?" My voice is wobbly.

"Not as good as I was expecting," he says. "It's hard being chronically ill and a guy."

"It's hard being chronically ill, full stop," I say.

He pulls another face. "Yeah, but … I don't know. Like I know women aren't often believed and men get taken more seriously, like if you've got to go to the emergency room and stuff. But this new doc today, she was just telling me to *man up*."

"Seriously?" I lean forward. Pain shoots down my spine.

Raymond nods, frustration clear in the lines on his forehead. "And I guess when most chronic illness patients are female, it does make me stand out a bit... even though Lyme affects both genders equally. But it's like docs just have this assumption that women are *more* chronically ill? That it's like a female space? I don't know how to explain it. I mean, it's not the first time a doc's had that attitude toward me. Doesn't hurt any less though. And I mean looking at me, a big Black guy, you wouldn't expect me to be feeling sick and weak, right?"

"I'm sorry you've had that experience," I say. "It really sucks."

"It does." He laughs, but I know that laugh and it's not a positive one. "Anyway, that's enough of us feeling sorry for ourselves. What've you got planned this week? Any new pages for the comic?"

I try to concentrate on my drawings, my art, try to talk to Raymond about it, but my heart's just not in it now. I can't concentrate on it. Only my illness—and how I've only got another three months of money left for treatment. I've been trying not to think about what will happen when the money runs out.

I'm going to get worse again. I know it.

I always try not to think about the times the brain inflammation and Lyme have been really bad. How dark it can make me feel. How *hopeless*. Way more than it is now, and this is bad enough. But right before we decided to go privately, I really was at the end of my tether, suicidal. The memory of those feelings and thoughts are a black pit inside me. The fear of it happening again is enough to scare me so much that I have nightmares about it happening, and I wake up soaked in sweat, heart pounding, convinced that this world is all too difficult for me.

Dad arrives home, two days later than expected and a week since his last stay with us. Whenever Dad's here, we eat at the table. Sitting there, on a chair that I don't feel is safe, so close to my family—people who I know are safe, but the OCD tells me aren't—has me nearly shaking. But I have to do it. I have to try and be normal. Dad wants to see progress being made. Wants to know that him and mum selling their shares of the family business was worth it, else he gets annoyed. So, I have to pretend I'm better. Or getting better, at least.

"Pass the salt, please," Dad says, eyes on me. He's got the same eyes as Esme, dark blue and piercing, the type that make you go cold if you look directly in them. I've got Mum's eyes—dark brown. But Mum's eyes look healthier than mine. There's life in hers.

I look toward the saltshaker, but Mum grabs it for me and slides it across the table to Dad. She always tries to help me like that.

Dad doesn't say anything, just seems to take forever grinding sea salt crystals onto his dinner. It's vegetable lasagna—what used to be my favorite. For dessert, we've got the strawberry mousse that Esme made in her food tech lesson earlier today. My stomach feels heavier just thinking about all that cream. I find dairy harder now, especially in large quantities.

"What film are we going to watch tonight?" Esme asks, shoveling lasagna into her mouth, because it's tradition that on the days Dad returns we all watch a film together after dinner.

My stomach roils at the hours I'll have to be brave for. The four of us crammed in the living room together—it's a small room. And Riley will be there too. Mum tries to keep him away from me, but last time he sniffed my foot and I panicked.

"You choose," Dad tells her, smiling.

He doesn't smile at me like that now, and it makes me cry. Because I've broken him, made him like this. My illness causes him stress, and he just wants me better, and I'm trying, but I can't get better quickly enough to please him.

SEVENTEEN

Cara

"HI." IT FEELS STRANGE talking to Damien on the phone the next day, knowing that he's interested in my best friend. That I blew my chance with him. That all I can be is his friend.

But a friend is better than nothing.

"All right?" he asks. His voice sounds richer on the phone, somehow, like a dial's been turned up.

"So, did you find a mutual friend with Marnie?"

I nod, then realize he won't know I've nodded. "Yep. Anastacia Hargreaves," I say. She and I never really got on at school. I was Jana's friend, not hers. It was only really River who flitted between our group and Anastacia's. Jana and Anastacia had this huge rivalry thing going on because they're cousins and apparently that means they have to compete. I was surprised when Anastacia invited me to her birthday celebrations. Very surprised, given I don't think I've said more than ten words to her since we left school. I hope it won't be awkward if Damien and I end up talking to her.

"Related to Jana?" Damien asks, and I hear the way his tone lightens as he says her name.

"Cousin," I say, and I don't want to talk about Jana. "So, I also saw on Facebook that Anastacia's been tagged in a lot of photos with Marnie. They're from a year ago, but maybe they were friends."

Damien makes a sound deep in his throat. "Great. We can question her about Marnie then."

"Question her? It's not an interrogation," I say, but just the thought of doing some sort of police role-play thing where Damien and I are playing good-cop-bad-cop, working together, has my heart pounding.

Damien laughs. "I know. But that is our goal, to get questions answered. Hmm. I wonder if maybe you should stick to questioning Anastacia and I go straight for Trevor—he's trying to get media attention, right? So, he's not going to be suspicious if a reporter visits him, right?"

My eyebrows shoot up. "You're going to pretend to be a reporter? He'll see right through you when you're not attached to a paper."

"Can still try," he says. "Can even set up some kind of online blog."

My mouth dries. "Well, okay then. Um…" I blink and look around my room. "I think we should also walk that last dog-walk route too that she took."

My mouth gets even drier at the thought of another walk with Damien. A walk where we're so close, just the two of us. And in the safety of my room it's easy to forget that in such a scenario my OCD would be going crazy. That I'd constantly be on high-alert, trying to avoid brushing against Damien or any trees or whatever. But in my imagination, I haven't got OCD—Damien and I would hug, and we'd both feel it, the connection we had in Mallorca, because we'd know it hadn't gone away, and then he'd realize it's me he wants to be with, not Jana.

But what am I doing, trying to ruin my best friend's happiness? Jana would be devastated if she knew.

"Already done it," he says.

"You have?" I grip the phone harder. "Did you find anything?"

"No. But I didn't expect to, not really. Tends to only be forensics that find things at the scene, right? So." He clears his throat. "Can you talk to Anastacia today?"

"I'm not sure when she's working."

"Where does she work?"

"Post office," I say. I blink. It's Friday. I think she works Fridays.

"We can call in there today," Damien says. "And I can check in with Trevor, too. I've found his address."

"You have?"

"Media contact page on his blog," he says. I hear him exhale. "And he'll be home today. Works from home most of the time for his firm, anyway. Actually, can you come with me when I'm seeing Trevor?"

"With you?" My voice is breathless.

"Looking inside Marnie's room could be helpful. You know, some abduction victims know their abductors. Could be an ex. Would also be helpful to look at Marnie's laptop."

"Uh, how will you manage that?"

"Well, if you're talking to Trevor, I can slip upstairs."

My heart pounds. "Damien, that's too risky. And illegal?"

"It's what all the detectives do on the true crime programs though. So, can we meet outside the post office in a couple hours?" he asks. "Can interview Anastacia, then we can go from there."

I meet Damien at the planned time outside the post office. He waves and smiles, doesn't attempt a hug. I breathe a sigh of relief. My head's pounding, and I'm feeling the effects of the Lyme more now than when I first got up. It's a general light-headedness that threatens to get heavier.

"Just strike up a casual conversation," he tells me. "And then see if you can steer it to Marnie and her exes. Exes—or current partners—are responsible for a lot of cases like this."

I nod, but my stomach's tightening and the nerves are making me sick.

"You can do it," he says. And he grins at me. It is a grin that is heart-stopping, that reminds me exactly why I fell for Damien in the first place. "And then we can go to Trevor's together."

Together. I like the way he says it.

I nod at him. "Okay. Let's do this."

Inside the post office it's cool and smells faintly of perfume. I wrinkle my nose, knowing the scent will be enough to make my headache worsen. Anastacia's at the counter and I saunter up. Damien's behind me, but when I turn to look up at him, I find he's now apparently fascinated by something on one of the aisles—holding a shoe spray so intently that says it can cure 'even the smelliest of feet.' I realize he's not actually registered what it is he's picked up, he's just trying to look nonchalant.

I try not to laugh.

"Can I help you?" Anastacia's voice is low, kind of husky. It's similar to Jana's, except my best friend has more intonation in her voice. Her words are nearly always melodic and chirpy.

I turn back quickly. "Uh, yeah." I grab the nearest item—a bottle of water to the side of the counter. "Just this please."

My heart's pounding, least of all because I've touched the water bottle. I dig my bank card out of my pocket. How am I going to bring up Marnie? I look around, feel my face reddening.

"You haven't got any posters up in here for Marnie?" I ask, even though I can see that they haven't.

Anastacia shrugs. "Why would we? She ran away." She rings up the till.

"So, you believe that?" I ask, and oh my god, how obvious am I being?

Anastacia regards me carefully, her painted red lips narrowing. "Why are you concerned all of a sudden? It's been nearly three weeks since she ran away."

Damien's now to my right, sort of parallel to the counter, and I can tell he's concentrating solely on me and not what's actually on the shelf he's pretending to look at, because now he's picking another of the items up without looking at it—a headlice comb. The corners of my lips twitch and I have to concentrate on focusing back on Anastacia. Anastacia—who's waiting for an answer from me.

"I… I was just wondering," I say. I look to Damien for help, and he's mouthing something at me.

What? I squint at him.

Anastacia clears her throat, and I jump, turn and look at her.

"Is there anything else I can help you with?" she asks.

"Yes," Damien says suddenly. "Uh, Cara's just a little nervous to ask you. But, basically, this is a bit awkward, what with Marnie being missing and all."

Anastacia watches him through narrowed eyes, her lips pursed together.

"So, you know Marnie's ex?" Damien leans against the counter. He's still holding the headlice comb. "Well, he's asked Cara to go out for a drink with him and she's a bit nervous, doesn't really know him. But, seeing as you know Marnie, we thought you might know her ex too?"

Anastacia's gaze lands on me. "Her *ex*?"

"Yeah, we thought you might know him?" Damien gives her a smile.

"Him?" She raises her eyebrows. "Marnie's into *women*."

I feel the color drain from my face and I shoot dagger looks at him. This is far from subtle.

"Sorry, who are you again?" Anastacia fixes Damien with a pensive glare.

"He's a friend of mine," I say quickly.

Anastacia frowns. "Why are you lying to me about this? And why are you interested?"

I wring my hands together, nearly dropping my newly purchased bottle of water. "Sorry, we were just trying to get information," I say, just as Damien says, "No reason."

I groan inwardly.

"We were just curious, that's all."

"Curious to make up a date that Cara's apparently going on?" Anastacia raises her eyebrows. "Cara—who doesn't date?"

Who doesn't date?

I stare at her. "I do date."

She laughs. "Hard to do that when you rarely leave the house."

"I was at your birthday celebrations."

She snorts. "And that just proves that you rarely get out. No one says 'birthday celebrations' now. So, what's going on?" Her eyes cross to Damien. "And who is this guy? You got nits?"

Damien realizes he's holding the headlice comb and drops it on the floor. "No," he says as he picks it up quickly, then puts it back on the shelf. I cringe, imagining the poor person who buys it next, who'll run it through their hair not knowing that it's touched the dirty floor in the shop.

"We just wanted a lead," I mumble. "We thought we could help find Marnie."

I can't tell what Anastacia's thinking as she stares at me, her face expressionless. "Well, good luck finding her."

"Aren't you worried?" Damien asks her. "You're friends with her?"

Anastacia shrugs. "I'd be worried if I thought something had happened. But it hasn't."

"Trevor thinks it has."

She rolls her eyes. "Of course he does. He doesn't want to accept that his perfect sister is messed-up."

"Messed up?" Damien asks.

"She's in that wild phase," Anastacia says. "But she'll be back soon. Once she's calmed down. Now, if you're not going to buy anything else, please leave."

"Well, that went well," I mutter once we're outside the shop.

"Yeah, you're a natural." Damien gives me an amused look, then winks.

I laugh and smile, and so does he.

"Well, we got some info," he says. "Marnie's into women. Hmm. Most crimes of passion are committed by men, but still, any lover can do it."

He steps closer to me, and my alarm bells go off again. I find myself stepping away quickly.

Damien notices. The tips of his ears redden.

"So, are we going to Trevor's now?" I ask.

He nods. "Yes. It's that way."

Damien always was amazing at memorizing maps and routes—that's something I remember strongly about the retreat. For one of the challenges, we were dropped off on the mountainside above Deià, and we had to navigate to the meeting point. We were in groups of four—it was me and Damien and Jana and Ray—and we won, all thanks to Damien. He's like a human compass.

My heart pounds as we walk.

"I've got a date with Jana on Monday," Damien tells me after we've crossed the road.

"I know," I say. "She told me." Even if I'd been trying to pretend that it wouldn't actually happen.

His eyes are wide. "You…you're okay with it?"

Me? He's worried about me not being okay with it? *Of course* I'm not. I want to scream and tell him *I* want to be with him.

But I know that wouldn't be fair.

Not when I can't even hug him.

"Of course," I say, and I try to make my voice light and casual, but my words don't ring true.

Damien nods once, then clears his throat. "Right."

I tell myself that I'm wrong when I sense disappointment in his voice. Because he can't actually be disappointed? No, that's just me projecting my own feelings on him. No one going out with Jana would be disappointed.

EIGHTEEN

Damien

"HELLO!" I OFFER my hand to Trevor within a second of him opening the door.

He's a tall man with very thick eyebrows, and a dusting of flour clings to one side of his face. His skin is a lot darker than Marnie's—I think he's mixed race, whereas in the photos she looks like she's white—and he's eyeing me warily. He's also holding a mixing bowl, full of some sort of batter, with a large, wooden spoon sticking out of it.

"Oh, what are you making?" I ask. I love a spot of baking. My stomach rumbles at the thought of my brother's homemade Victoria sponge. That man can cook.

"Uh, who are you?" Trevor regards me with confusion.

"Oh, I'm Damien," I say, and I'm speaking fast because I'm nervous—because he's going to see this through as quickly as Anastacia did? "And this is…" I turn to introduce Cara, but then find she's several feet behind me. She looks worried. "This is Cara."

Trevor inclines his head slightly. "Okay, but what are you doing at my door?"

"We're reporters," I say, my voice light and cheery. "We saw your campaign about your sister, Marnie, is it? And we wanted to chat with you."

Trevor readjusts the mixing bowl in his arms. "Reporters? Where from?"

I open my mouth to answer, but of course I suddenly am tongue-tied and can't think of a word.

"We're making a podcast," Cara says from behind me.

A podcast! Why didn't I think of that? I stare at her, but she's already continuing.

"It's, uh, a series where each episode looks at a different disappearance."

"Yeah?" Trevor asks. "What's it called?"

"*Damien the Detective*," Cara says before I can even think of anything. And the way she says my name, pronouncing each syllable in 'Damien' so richly, makes my heart pound. "That's the series name, so each episode would have its own subtitle too, specific to the missing person."

She speaks like we've really planned this all out. Wait—has she already planned out a podcast? I glance back at her, and her eyes on me. They look bright now, and I want to move closer to her. Want to hug her, just as we hugged plenty of times on the retreat.

Trevor clears his throat, and I turn back to him. He looks us up and down. "Okay..." But he says the word as if it's more of a question, as if he's trying to work out whether we're playing at this or not. I don't blame him.

"We're a very small podcast," I say. "Full disclosure. I mean, this would be for our first episode. But we want to help you find Marnie."

Man, he's not going to talk to us, I'm sure of it. And I'm about to accept that fact—and just how bad Cara and I really are at this detective work—when Trevor steps slightly to the side.

"Better having you than no one," he says. "Come in. I'll fill you in on everything."

Trevor's house is messy. Clothes everywhere, in stacks on counters and draped over chairs. Picture books lie open, scattered across the carpet.

"Sorry about the mess," he says. "You mind if I finish making these? Cupcakes for Vivi, my daughter. I've got to collect her from nursery soon."

I look up at the wall where I see many photos of a chubby toddler with the most cheerful smile I've ever seen.

"How old is she?" Cara asks.

I turn and see the way Cara's looking at the photos of Vivi. There's a sense of wonder in her eyes, and she looks happy, smiling softly to herself, as she looks at the photos. It actually brings a bit of color into her face—and it's strange how memories are different to real life. Because Cara looks pale most of the time, I've noticed that, yet when we were in Mallorca, I don't remember her looking pale. There, she just seemed more…vibrant.

"Three. Tomorrow," Trevor says, heading to the island in the kitchen side of the open-plan kitchen-lounge room. "Take a seat."

There's one sofa that's not absolutely covered with clothes, so I perch on one end of it, leaving space for Cara. She looks at it nervously for several seconds. Her hands are shaking. I'm about to ask her what's wrong when she sits down, her back impeccably straight. She doesn't lean against the cushions as I do.

"So, Marnie wanted to be an influencer, right?" I ask.

Trevor stares at me for a moment. "You've done your research."

"Her Instagram's open to the public," I say.

He nods. "It's all she's wanted to be, ever since she was fourteen. I mean, she wanted to be famous ever since I've known her."

"Since you've known her?"

"Our parents adopted her when she was six. Even then, she was the same—though she thought she'd be a singer, at that age singing was all she'd talk about. But then as she got older, it became all about this influencer stuff. And she'd started to get somewhere—so that's why I know she wouldn't just run away right now. Not like this. And especially not halfway through a dog walk. She's missing."

I try to concentrate on what Trevor's saying—and I should be concentrating, I know that, because this is a case. This is an actual case. But Cara's sitting so close to me. Her thigh is inches away from mine, and of course it's making me think of all the times we sat together, legs brushing each other's, on the retreat.

I inhale deeply, trying to clear my thoughts and focus on Trevor and why we're actually here in the first place. Because this is my first actual crime a case. A missing girl. But a waft of Cara's shampoo wafts over me and I'm inhaling it, inhaling *her*. It's coconut, not citrus like in Mallorca.

I look over to the other wall and see a family photo: Marnie, Trevor, two other adults in their twenties who I assume are more siblings, along with an elderly man who's got his arm around Trevor.

"So, can we have a look around her room?" I ask.

Trevor pauses, his hand hovering above his mixing bowl. "A quick look. But I'll come with you. Just wait a second. I want to get this in the oven."

I try to make small talk with Cara as Trevor pours the cake batter into cupcake cases lined up on a tray, but Cara's all one-word answers now. She's gone even paler, and her hands are gripped tightly together in her lap.

"You okay?" I whisper, leaning closer to her.

She nods. Doesn't look at me. Just stays rigid.

"Cara?"

"I'm fine," she says, tight-lipped, and then Trevor's heading back over to us, wiping his hands on his apron. It's got cartoon ducks on it.

"My daughter's choice," he says, noticing me looking. "Anyway, come on. Marnie's room is upstairs."

We head up. The house is surprisingly big. Trevor explains that there are four siblings, including Marnie, but only he and Marnie still live here. The oldest brother moved out a few years ago, and the youngest sister lives with their mother. She's in Belarus, where that side of their family is from. Trevor's elderly father also lives here, but he's out playing golf today. Most days, in fact. The house has three floors, and there's even a home gym, and a playroom for Trevor's daughter.

"This is Marnie's." Trevor swings open a door.

I don't know what I was expecting to see, but it looks exactly like any other young woman's room. Or at least what I think any other young woman's room would look like.

I try not to wonder what Cara's room looks like.

"Anything in particular you want to look at?" Trevor asks.

"Has she got a laptop?" Cara asks.

"Of course." Trevor points to the desk.

"Can we have a look."

"Password protected," he says.

"Can't the police get past that?"

Trevor laughs. "They could if they were interested enough to think of it. So, you haven't got any PI skills?"

"We're very new," I say, glancing at Cara. She looks even paler still, and she's swaying slightly. Then she sees me looking at her and turns away, apparently fascinated by the view out of Marnie's window.

"So, she hasn't taken any clothes or anything with her?" I ask Trevor.

"Nope—which proves this wasn't planned, this 'runaway.'" He puts air-quotes around the last word. "And it's not like she was having a particularly rough time right now either," he says. "I mean, she'd started her own business—way better than that temporary waitressing job she had, and she was enjoying it. Plus, her influence stuff was taking off. And she adored Vivi. No," he says. "Something's happened. And I need people to take this seriously."

I almost feel bad for him that he's got us, me and Cara, two amateurs. Because even though I'm fascinated by true crime I realize I haven't got a clue what to do. Shame fills me, but I bluster on, trying to think of anything and everything to ask.

Half an hour later, Cara and I leave Trevor's. He thanks us for our time and gives us a handful of missing posters of Marnie to put up.

As we walk away, Cara's quiet and looking even more pale than I thought was physically possible.

"Are you okay?" I ask her.

She nods.

"We made good progress, right?" I say, but I know we haven't. We haven't got any leads. Marnie just disappeared. "We just need to decide what we're going to do now."

"Now?" she asks.

I nod.

"Well, we'd better actually set up that podcast. *Damien the Detective.*" She glances at me quickly, as if looking for approval. Her nose has gone pink, and there's another emotion in her eyes, other than her search for approval. An emotion I can't decipher.

But I'm not really trying to, because she said my name again—and I don't know what it is about my name on her lips, but it just cements everything that I've been feeling for her. Makes it so much stronger. Makes me feel bad about seeing Jana on Monday.

"We could start with just a simple blog," she suggests. "Put up some info about it. Make it seem like we're actually legit. No idea how to actually record a podcast though. Do you?"

"Uh," I say, my heart thumping. I do know—I looked it up years ago, but I can't even think of the words to say right now. I'm just hooked on the idea of producing a podcast with Cara, of spending so much more time with her. And she must want to, too?

I lean in closer to her—and it's like I've struck her with lightning or something. She jumps right back. Hurt flashes through me.

Cara hugs her arms around her body, looking at the chewing-gum-stained tarmac beneath our feet. "I've got to get home now," she says. "Sorry."

She doesn't wait for me to say anything, just scurries off.

I stare after her as she leaves, her figure getting smaller and smaller until she disappears around the corner. I try to pretend like my heart's not breaking as she walks away. She couldn't make it clearer that she's not interested in me if she tried.

So, why was she smiling and laughing with me earlier, after we finished at the post office? Why did she make it seem like we really would be making our podcast?

NINETEEN

Cara

"IT'S LIKE WE'RE the only people in the world right now," I say, drinking in the tranquility of the forest. And it's quiet—save for the whispering of the leaves and the slight whirring sound of some insects. But that's all I can hear, that and my own beating heart, because the sounds of the others out searching for the treasure have disappeared. It's just me and Damien, right now. Because this is a special place, a place just for us, this little haven of soft amber light from the setting sun, between the trees.

Right now, nothing else exists.

Damien smiles as he nods. We're standing close, so close, and I want to reach for his hand. Want to lace my fingers through his. I just want to be close, and I can't describe the enormity of the feeling, the way it drinks me up completely, because I've never felt like this before. Never felt so…connected.

And then he's moving toward me, eradicating the space between us. His arms wrap around me, and I lean into him. My ear goes against his chest, and I listen to the reassuring thump-thump-thump of his heart. It's grounding, so grounding. I've never felt safer.

"I like you, Cara," he says, and his words are so low I nearly miss him speaking. Because everything inside me is screaming with excitement

and disbelief—that this is Damien Noelle, and I'm in his arms, and he's chosen me to be out here with, me to be with…

Because this is what it is, right?

I look up at him, my heart pounding. Is this it? Is this where he kisses me? My first ever kiss…

Damien smiles, and his eyes are doing that jumpy thing that my own do when I'm nervous—when I can't decide what to look at so I just keep looking at different things, one after another, never able to settle. But Damien can't be nervous, can he? He's a guy—he's supposed to lead in situations like this. Then I realize how stupid that sounds. Of course guys can be nervous.

I am, so why wouldn't Damien be?

I swallow hard, my fingers feeling all strange. I glance at his eyes, at the exact same moment he looks at me. Chills run through me at the direct eye contact. It's intense, like I'm staring into his soul, like he can see every hidden part of me. Like there are no secrets between us.

"Anyone still out here?" Mrs. Mitchell's voice travels through the fog.

Damien and I spring apart.

"We'd better get back," he says, and I nod, give him a smile.

We exchange nervous smiles every few seconds, all the way back.

TWENTY

Damien

MONDAY, THE 2nd of October, flies around all too soon, and nerves fill me the moment I wake up. I walk Rufus, still my only client, and then all too soon it's the afternoon and it's time for my date with Jana.

Today, I'm going out with *Jana.* I concentrate on that, not Cara. Not on how I replayed all of yesterday over and over in the night, trying to work out if I have upset Cara.

Jana Hargreaves.

And part of me almost can't believe it. Jana is going on a date with me. Me!

On the dating holiday, Jana was the plucky girl that everyone around me was talking about. In all the team events, everyone wanted to be paired up with her. I mean, I didn't because I was enamored with Cara, but now I can see exactly what the appeal of Jana is. She's bubbly and energetic—her enthusiasm is contagious. She's just so smiley—I never quite noticed that before.

Jana has a car, so she picks me up, and I think of all the jokes my brother would be making about this. Luke's proper old-fashioned and stereotypical. *The man should always pick the woman up.*

"Nice car," I say to Jana as I get in her Peugeot.

"Thanks." Her voice is chirpy today. Almost like she's singing. "So, have you decided where we're going, or do I get to choose?" Her eyes sparkle as she looks across the console at me.

"Is there somewhere you want to go?" I ask.

"The moors!" Her eyes glisten. "I can show you my favorite part of Dartmoor."

"This would be an *amazing* place to walk the dogs," I say, breathless, as I stare at the tors in front of us. "You know, I walk dogs for a living?" I look at Jana.

"I can always drive you all up here." She laughs. "Just wait until you see the view at the top of there." She points at the nearest tor.

It doesn't take us long to walk up there—only about forty minutes—and as we walk, I know for sure that I'm not a city guy. This, being out here, is what I was made for. Being in nature. I'm in my element.

"We should've brought a picnic," Jana says as we reach the top. She shields her eyes from the sun. "Wow, what a view."

But the mention of the picnic makes me think of Cara. Of how the two of us had a picnic on that last day of the retreat. It was a non-timetabled day, that last one. Everyone else was going to the beaches or off to buy souvenirs. But not me and Cara…

The light is golden, so perfect, framing Cara's face perfectly. Her hair looks more golden, lighter in this light, and I reach across, brush her hair away from her face. The back of my hand brushes her skin, and electric shocks jolt through me.

This girl! This girl is the one. I can just tell. I mean, I suspected it before, when we just clicked. But last night, last night, hugging her as the sunset around us, with all the trees as our guards, that was when I knew.

She starts laughing.

"What?" I ask her, smiling.

"Nothing," she says, but her laughter is infectious.

Nervous, we're both nervous, sitting out here, on the ragged mountainside above Valldemossa, a picnic of the food we'd managed to save from the breakfast buffet spread out between us.

And in this moment, I know I never want to leave. Because this is perfection—with Cara. So long as we're together, it just feels like everything will be okay.

I focus back on Jana, feel slightly jarred at the way the memory suddenly came back to me. It was like I was there. I can smell Cara's perfume now.

I shake my head, trying to clear it.

Stop it, I tell myself. I'm on a date with Jana now. And Cara's not interested. I mean, it's like she's a completely different person now.

I take a deep breath. Jana's talking—something about a book she's writing that's set on Dartmoor—and I tell myself to concentrate. But of course as soon as I tell myself to do that, I do the opposite. I think of Cara, and I try to work out what happened.

Did I upset her somehow? Either yesterday or earlier in the week, or even three years ago?

Was it a misunderstanding? Did she think she'd given me her number and she was waiting for me to call her?

But, no, I remember it clearly. On the last day of the retreat, when we were allowed our phones again and contact with the outside world, Cara's phone wouldn't charge. Her charger had broken and she couldn't turn her phone on. She'd got a new number recently, she'd said, and she didn't know it off by heart then. So, I wrote my number down for her—on the inside cover of the novel she was reading, written in pencil of course. I'm not a monster.

No, she could've called me.

She just didn't. And I even told her about my date today with Jana yesterday. If she was interested in me, that was the perfect chance to say something. And she didn't.

I've got to move on.

"I'm stopping off at this library," Jana says on the way back, a few hours later. "It's bigger than Brackerwood's. Want to come in?"

"Sure." We're in her car, and I'm surprised by how tired I am—after climbing that first tor we climbed two others—but I want to get to know Jana. Does she like reading too? Just like Cara?

I swallow hard and steer my thoughts away from her.

Jana pulls her car into a parking space outside a huge, red-brick building with tall, arching windows of tinted glass.

We get out. There's a cool breeze setting in now, and we hurry inside.

This library is huge. Jana's right—it's definitely bigger than the one I saw her and her friends in last week. This one has shelves that seem to go on for miles. It's the kind of library that makes me think of spooky stories being told in candlelight, where the flickering flame lights up the books around it.

"Oh, that's Esme," Jana says. "You remember Cara? That's her little sister."

Cara's *sister.* I go cold suddenly, and I don't know why. Because looking at the girl, who so obviously looks like Cara, is making me think of her. Someone who's not interested in me. Why am I thinking of her when I'm with a woman who *is* interested in me?

"Hey, Es," Jana calls out. "Is Cara here too?"

"She still won't come here," Esme says, rolling her eyes. "Says it's too dangerous."

Too dangerous? I frown, but Jana's not reacting to Esme's words with puzzlement or confusion. She just nods.

"You here on your own?"

"I'm thirteen now." Esme folds her arms and gives what has to be the most sassy glare I've ever seen. "Anyway, Cara and Mum are still at the hospital."

"The hospital?" My eyes widen. "Is everything okay?"

"Everything apart from Cara's brain," Esme says.

Jana gives her a look. "It's not her fault—she's ill."

"I know, I know!" Esme looks annoyed. "It just takes up so much time. All the time. Mum was supposed to get back here—my story's being read out in..." She turns and looks at the clock on the wall. "Seven minutes. But Mum texted half an hour ago, and they're still in Exeter. Still *waiting* for the appointment. It hasn't even started yet. They're going to miss my story."

"Your story?" Jana asks.

"I won the creative writing competition for Devon Libraries. And Mum and Cara were going to hear it being read out." Sadness fills her eyes. "And get my prize too."

"Well we can stay, can't we?" Jana looks at me and I nod. "Esme, this is Damien, he's a friend. But we'll hear your story being read out. And you getting your prize too. Then we can tell Cara and your mum all about it."

Esme doesn't look any happier about it, but she nods. "Okay."

"Hey, what's wrong with Cara?" I ask Jana in a low voice. "Has she got a brain injury or something?" I can't keep the alarm out of my voice.

"She's got brain inflammation," she tells me.

Brain inflammation?

"Come on, it's starting!" Esme says, and she grabs Jana's sleeve and hauls her toward the front of the library.

I follow.

"But is she okay?" I ask Jana in a whisper.

"No talking." A librarian shoots me a glance.

It's close to agony, sitting through the readings while I know that something is wrong with Cara, but not exactly what. The moment the last reading is over, I ask Jana again.

She looks uncomfortable. "She should probably tell you herself."

"But she doesn't want to see me." I shake my head. "Just…this brain inflammation, is it serious?"

Jana takes a deep breath. "I don't know, okay. She's sick, really sick, despite what some people think. She hides it as best as she can though. But, look, you should be asking her about this. Not me."

Ask Cara about it? But she doesn't want to see me.

Only what if I've got it wrong, and she does want to see me, but it's the illness—whatever exactly it is—making it difficult?

I think of the times recently when she's blown hot and cold on me. How one minute it would seem like we were connecting—really connecting—and then suddenly she'd changed. Was that her brain inflammation worsening then?

Oh, God. I never even asked her how she was. Like, that's that first thing you say to someone, isn't it? *How are you?* I wrack my brain, but I can't ever remember asking Cara this—not in a serious way that went beyond a quick greeting.

Now I think about it, Cara *has* looked ill. She's not been as vibrant as she was in Mallorca. I've noticed the bags under her eyes, how pale she's looked at times—especially on that trip to Trevor's. I asked her then if she was okay, but I didn't persist. Didn't text and ask her later. What if she thinks I wasn't interested in her enough to even notice that or ask her properly?

I groan. The roof of my mouth is dry.

I need to see her.

TWENTY-ONE

Cara

ACCORDING TO THE NHS, I am a hypochondriac. Therefore, I still have to see a psychiatrist regularly.

I haven't been looking forward to this next appointment with Dr. Fallon. Mum's here with me, because I know better now than to go to these alone. The ones I've attended with Dr. Fallon alone are the ones where he's bullied me—where I've left in tears. And crying in front of him only fuels his certainty that I am just an anxious/depressed/psychotic girl. Never a woman, according to him. Always a *girl*. And not in the friendly way Jana and River say it.

"This is going to be very distressing to hear," Dr. Fallon says. He sits in his swivel chair behind his desk and clasps his hands together in a steeple fashion. "And it is a difficult conversation to have. But as I have told you before, all these symptoms you are experiencing in your body are due to anxiety. You are so very traumatized that this is your mind's way of coping with it, projecting these ill feelings onto your body. Making you *think* you have got pain."

Dr. Fallon the Fake. Dr. Fallon the Fraud. Dr. Fallon the Foul.

"But I *have* got pain." I grit my teeth. I can't help myself. I shouldn't argue with him—but I need him to listen. Sooner or later, the money for the private treatment is going to run out, I know that. And Dr. Singh said it would take years—plural. My goal has always been that by the time my funding for private care is depleted that I'll somehow have managed to persuade the NHS to continue my treatment. Wishful thinking, I know, given practically no one in my online support group has managed this.

But I have to try. And maybe if I can get them to recognize my case of chronic Lyme, then they'd recognize others' cases too. More people would get help instead of being left to suffer needlessly. It's criminal, what they're currently doing.

Don't get me wrong, I'm not saying the NHS is all bad. It's great for emergencies, broken legs, that sort of thing. It's just their line of reasoning when they can't find the answer is wrong: if they don't know what it is, they say it doesn't exist—it being a physical disorder—and tell you it's anxiety. If it's an illness that the NICE guidelines don't cover, they say it doesn't exist, that it's just your mind going wrong.

Something needs to change.

And, so, I have to keep up with these appointments. If I skip these psychiatrist sessions, I risk being refused NHS help later.

"Cara, you think you are in pain, but you're not."

"I am in pain," I persevere, and I picture the caricature of him I'm going to draw later—him, wearing cartoon jail clothes, and a top hat, and holding a sign that reads 'I am a fool.'

It's silly, but it's how I cope when people don't believe me. Before, I used to draw caricatures of everyone, and I'd make them funny and amusing. But now I've got a whole collection of these 'mean caricatures,' where I've drawn everyone who upsets me or tells me I'm wrong or imagining it all. Dr. Fallon features in the pile of them a lot. As do many of the NHS doctors—not all of them though. Some are nice.

"Right now, I have got kidney pain," I say to Dr. Fallon. I mean, I could reel off a whole bunch other body parts that hurt—my neck is stiff, my lower back is throbbing, my left hip is painful—but I know there's no point in that.

Dr. Fallon leans back in his chair. a wistful look takes over his eyes. "The kidneys are a funny thing."

Yes, the kidneys are hilarious.

I give him a blunt look, or what I hope is a blunt look.

"You can feel pain in your kidneys even when your kidneys are fine—as blood tests have shown you."

"But blood tests have also shown I've got Lyme."

"The NHS blood test was clear for that."

The NHS blood test isn't reliable.

"It is very sad when this happens to a young girl, such as yourself—when a girl has tricked herself into believing she is very ill, so much so she even feels the pain she is reporting. Pain that is in the mind, but she feels it in...her kidneys." He gives me what I think is supposed to be a sympathetic look, but it just gets under my skin. My blood feels too hot. "This happens to people when their minds are greatly unwell. They convince themselves they have a physical disorder, but they do not."

"So why do antibiotics improve my OCD and physical symptoms if there's nothing physical it's treating?" *Like Lyme disease.*

"Placebo effect. Because, my dear girl, you are just so desperate to be unwell."

"Desperate to be unwell?" I stare at him.

"She really does not want to be ill like this," Mum says.

"I think she does not even know that subconsciously this is what she's doing. But it's a reaction to trauma. Tell me, Cara, have you had any bad relationships?"

"Bad relationships?" I stare at him. How on earth is this relevant?

"A recent breakup can lead to feelings such as this—she pretends to be unwell in order to get sympathy." He gives my mum a knowing look.

"I've never had a relationship," I say.

Dr. Fallon's eyes light up. "Never?" He glances at Mum. Mum looks at him tight-lipped. She doesn't mention the date with Damien last week, thank God. "Well, well, well." Dr. Fallon chuckles in a sad, sad way. "This is exactly it. You are scared of sexual relations, and so you're trying to make yourself as unappealing as possible to potential sexual and romantic partners so that you don't have to face your fears."

"I'm sorry—what?" I nearly explode. And wow—I didn't even mention being ace. If I had, I can't even imagine what Dr. Know-It-All would have to say about that, because of course he'd have an opinion on it. and probably a very offensive one. "I have Lyme disease—that is why I am unwell. I have a private doctor who's *proven* it. I can show you the lab tests."

"You are so caught up in this illusion you're wasting thousands of pounds, chasing a diagnosis that is not yours."

A few choice words spring to mind, but I hold myself back from calling him them.

"So, what's the treatment you're suggesting then?" Mum asks. She looks at me and gives me a little nod. She's humoring him.

"Ah, treatment, yes." Dr. Fallon smiles. "So, I recommend that we hand over your case to the Community Mental Health Services so you can access weekly intensive therapy through them. I will also be prescribing you further medications—and make sure you take these ones."

"What medications?" Mum asks.

"Similar to the last ones."

So, antipsychotics then. The antipsychotics that Dr. Singh told me not to take because they'll make the brain inflammation worse.

I count down the minutes until the appointment is over, until I can escape and vent my frustration in the car.

TWENTY-TWO

Cara

I DON'T FEEL right as Mum and I travel back from the appointment, as we pick up Esme from the library, as Esme complains that we missed her story, as Mum tells her that we're both sorry. But I can't quite place what it is *wrong*—it's more than that disastrous appointment—and even by the time I'm safely up in my room, having showered, I still don't feel right. I just stare around my room. All I can tell is that I don't feel right and this room doesn't look right either. Nothing looks right. I frown and touch my head. My skin feels…different. Doesn't it?

I take a deep breath.

Maybe I'm just tired.

Yep. I just need to rest.

My eyes fall on the medications on my desk. So many of them. I need to take my next dose of Doxycycline though.

I swallow the pills hastily, still feeling strange. Still feeling like none of this is real.

Just sleep, a voice says.

So, I lie on my bed, and I sleep. I sleep and sleep until Mum shouts up the stairs that I've got a visitor.

A visitor? I open my eyes, groggy. My sight isn't quite right. I still feel strange.

At the bottom of the stairs, I come to an abrupt stop.

Damien is standing in my hallway.

I stare at him, half expecting him to just vanish before my eyes. Disappear—because he's a figment of my imagination. He has to be.

But he doesn't vanish.

If anything, he seems to get more real.

"Hi," I say. My voice sounds scratchy.

"Cara," he says, and just the way he says my name makes my legs weaken. Because he sounds the same as he did on the retreat, and those memories flood me.

Stop it, I tell myself. I ruined my chance with him. I can't have him. He's with Jana now anyway. Not me.

"How are you?" Damien asks.

How am I? I stare at him. My face is starting to sting. "Okay," I say.

He shakes his head. "Why didn't you tell me?"

"Tell you what?"

"That you're ill."

Ill. I hate that word. Like it's the only thing that defines me now—and the problem is, that's how it feels. It really does feel as if I'm only this illness now. It's consumed me, and maybe somewhere inside me the old me is still here, but all I feel now is the Lyme. I feel that that's the only thing that defines me. And, sure, Mum's always saying that's not true—and she'll talk about my art and how I still like crime fiction. But even those things just seem bland now in comparison to the all-consuming force that is this disease.

And I didn't want Damien to know about my illness. As if I could just pretend to be normal. My shoulders slacken.

"Jana told me a bit," he says. "But I… I don't understand?" He looks worried. "I had no idea you weren't well, Cara. I mean, if this is too much, just tell me." He gestures around my hallway.

"What?" I squint at him, confused.

"Do you need to sit down?"

"It's fine," I say.

Riley—apparently suddenly aware that Damien is here—barrels out of the kitchen and straight at Damien, who nearly falls over as fifty pounds of dog hits him. Damien makes an *oof* noise.

"Careful, boy." He laughs, but his laugh doesn't ring true. He looks up at me as he pacifies Riley. "Is it…is it serious? This illness?"

I take a deep breath. I hate this. Hate this conversation. Because it's where I'll just get an extra level of confirmation that he's not interested in me. I mean, he clearly isn't anyway, as he's taking Jana on dates.

Jana.

Suddenly, I picture the two of them kissing. It feels like a punch to the gut.

I swallow hard.

"Cara?" Damien prompts.

"I've got brain inflammation—because of Lyme disease." I look at my feet, then up at him when he doesn't say anything.

His eyes are wide. In my hallway, they don't look as blue. They look duller somehow—or maybe it's me. Maybe I'm sucking the life out of him, just like this illness is sucking the life out of me.

"Isn't that serious?" he asks.

I nod. "It affects pretty much everything."

"What is it then? Like, if I look it up, what do I google? Just brain inflammation?"

He wants to look it up? I frown a little. The roof of my mouth is suddenly too dry.

"Well, the brain stuff is autoimmune encephalitis," I say. "Encephalitis means brain inflammation. And I've got Lyme disease. Borrelia is the bacteria that causes Lyme. The encephalitis developed because the Lyme was treated."

"En—what?"

"Encephalitis." I swallow hastily. "Um, it's also known as PANS—that's easier to remember. Though it's mainly in children when it's called PANS. The P in Pans stands for Pediatric. Pediatric Acute-onset Neuropsychiatric Syndrome—but it's pretty much the same thing as encephalitis. And PANS and encephalitis can have a lot of causes, not just Lyme."

"Neuropsychiatric?" Damien takes a step back. Riley whines at him because he's stopped fussing him.

And here it comes. The fear. The backing away. Because no one wants to be taking to a crazy girl. Much less *be* with one—really, what was I thinking anyway? As if Damien's going to profess his love for me when he's seeing my best friend.

"Yeah," I say. "As in the symptoms it causes are neurological and psychiatric—because the brain is inflamed. So, I fall over, struggle with handwriting, and on bad days I can't speak. And I have OCD because of it." I decide not to mention my hallucinations. There's too much stigma around those.

"OCD." Damien nods. "Right. Okay. Like wanting to be neat and tidy?"

"No. As in a severe anxiety disorder that causes so much mental torment." My tone is blunt. I hate explaining the OCD. "I panic with touching anything. Anyone."

"Anyone?" He raises his eyebrows. "Oh." His eyes do a jumpy little thing, like he can't decide where to look. "So, it wasn't that *you* didn't want to hug me before? Just that it scared you, with the OCD?"

I nod, and I feel stupid and embarrassed, and I always feel like this when people try and talk about it to me. When I'm making my cartoon, it's different—I'm in control of the conversation then, and yeah, sometimes I do include stuff on chronic illness then. But not now. Now, this conversation could go anywhere, and I've got no warning.

"Shit," he says. "I'm sorry."

"You've got nothing to be sorry for."

"I had no idea."

I shift my weight to my other foot. "Like I said, you've got nothing to apologize for."

He clears his throat. "So, um…" Then he pulls his hands through his hair. "Can I ask you something? Like, without sounding crazy?"

He's worried that *he's* the one who's going to sound crazy? I almost laugh, but I nod. "Go on."

"So… Look, I still like you, Cara. And I… I assumed you didn't after… I mean, you didn't call me after the retreat anyway—but was that because of this? Jana mentioned this brain stuff happened three years ago. Is that why you didn't call me?"

I take a deep breath. It would be so easy to blame it on that.

"I wish I called you," I say. "But that's not the reason—I didn't get Lyme until a couple months later. "But I was scared—that's why I didn't call you."

"Scared?" He looks confused. "Of me?"

"Of things being different between us back here—like, it was amazing in Mallorca. And I wanted that, but I was just sure it couldn't be like that. I wanted to pick up the phone so many times, but I was scared, nervous. I just… I chickened out—then I lost the book with your number in." I look down. "I'd never had a boyfriend before—I still haven't. And I just… I'm scared." I laugh, but it sounds forced, even to my ears. "I mean it's probably for the best, otherwise you'd have a girlfriend now who couldn't even touch you."

Riley makes another whining sound.

"So, you do like me?" Damien sounds uncertain. "Because, look, I like you."

I nod. "I like you, yeah." Of course I do. "I didn't stop."

He doesn't say anything, and suddenly I'm aware of just how awkward this is. I clear my throat.

"But you're with Jana now," I say.

"It's been one date," he says. His eyes seem to drink me up. "But it's you I really like, Cara. It always has been you."

He's staring at me, waiting for me to say something. What can I say? Something that ruins Jana's happiness? But if he doesn't really like her, it's not fair for her to be strung along.

"I'm not the same person now," I say. "I was healthy then, fun. I'm not now. I'm boring, ill."

"You're not boring, Cara."

"You don't know me now," I laugh. "I am boring."

"You're not." He looks at me and it's a deep look, one that climbs right inside me. "You're still interested in true crime. You still love to draw. You're still the same person. You're still you."

"But I'm different now," I finally say.

"Then I want to know you," he says. "Please? Look, if you still feel anything, like I do, I think we have to try."

"But my OCD—"

"We can find a way around it. Or just not touch or anything."

"Not touch?" I shake my head. "Damien, that's not fair on you."

He steps closer toward me. The light in his eyes changes a little. I see hope in them. His hope. "Cara, what we have is too special to give up on. Yeah, you've got OCD now, but we can work around it. I promise—it's you I want to get to know. Please, can we try?"

I nod.

He brings his hand up to his mouth, pressing his palm against his lips. At first, I think he's yawning, but then I realize what he's actually doing: blowing me a kiss.

"There, for you," he says.

I can't help but smile.

"I've got to go now. Got a walk booked." He looks around a little uncertainly. "But I'll message you, okay?"

"Okay." I am smiling, even after he's gone, because I can almost 'feel' his kiss.

TWENTY-THREE

Jana

"HE DIDN'T EVEN try to kiss me yesterday." I shake my head as I stare at Lizzy, then I tie my apron strings behind my back. There's a huge stain on the front of my apron from before my break, where I was trying to clean the coffee machine earlier and part of it exploded. Bet Mr. Richards is going to have a go at me about that. Got to look presentable for the customers.

"But you're both ace anyway?" Lizzy frowns.

"Doesn't mean we can't kiss. Ace people can kiss if they want to."

"So, does he want to?" Lizzy asks. "Like, did you ask him if kissing is okay with him?"

"No, I didn't ask him." I sigh. I mean, asking that would've sounded ridiculous. And so forward too.

"Text him," Lizzy tells me. "Ask him on another date."

"You can do your socializing after work," Mr. Richards bellows. "I don't pay you to stand about, idly chatting about whatever nonsense is filling up your heads."

I glare at him.

Later, I mouth at Lizzy.

Yes, I'll text Damien later. I smile to myself.

There aren't many customers in today, and thankfully my next two order pots of tea rather than coffee so I don't have to wrestle with the machine again.

As Lizzy and I work, Mr. Richards keeps that hawk eye of his on us. Twice, I see him looking at Lizzy's cleavage. Each time, she pretends not to notice.

The bell rings as the door opens again, and a man steps in. He's mixed race, well over six foot, with dark hair and a way of moving that just screams urgency. Within a second of opening the door, he's clocked me and leapt toward me so quickly and with so much vigor that I nearly drop the teapot I'm holding.

"Have you seen her?" The man holds up a piece of paper inches from my face. I lean back a bit, heart pounding, as my eyes focus. It's a printed photo of Marnie Wathem. I look back at the man and I think recognize him from some appeal I saw on TV. Maybe her brother? Damn. What was his name? I can't remember.

"No, sorry," I say. "I haven't seen her."

"No chatting to your friends," Mr. Richards's voice booms from behind me and I jump.

"She's helping me," the man says, curtly. "I'm looking for my sister." He moves toward Mr. Richards, shoving the photo of Marnie in front of him. "Have you seen her?"

Mr. Richards—with barely a look at the poster in the man's hands—barks, "No!"

The man moves to the nearest lot of tables, where an elderly man and two toddlers are sitting. "Have you seen this woman?"

The elderly man leans forward, squinting through his thick-lensed glasses. "She looks familiar," he says.

"But have you seen her?"

The elderly man frowns and then looks at me. I don't know why.

"Can I leave one of these here?" the man with the posters asks me, holding one out to me. "Marnie did used to work here. Not that she liked your boss."

My eyebrows shoot up. "She worked here?"

"Not for long."

Mr. Richards clears his throat and looks at the man as if he's a bit of dirt on his shoe. "You most certainly *cannot* leave a poster here. This is a respectable eating establishment. We don't want to be advertising teenagers who've made bad decisions."

"What?" The man looks like he's going to explode.

"But she used to work here," I say.

Mr. Richards sniffs. "And she was useless. I'm not surprised she's runaway—she was just the type."

All the customers are staring at Mr. Richards now.

"Of course you can leave a poster here," I say. "I'm sorry about him."

Mr. Richards shoots a dagger-look at me. "I am your boss. I make the decisions around here, not you."

"But there's a woman missing," Lizzy says. The whole time, she's kept quiet. But now she speaks in a furious whisper.

"So, you think you can challenge the way things are run in *my* shop?" Mr. Richards's nostrils flare. It makes him look like a toad.

"I'm not challenging you," Lizzy says. "But putting up a poster of a missing girl is just being a decent human being."

"A decent human being?" Mr. Richards shouts. "I've had enough of you girls! Thinking you can get away with anything because you're pretty. I employ you to serve my customers, not to decorate my walls with photos of runaway teens."

"She didn't run away," the man says. He's still clutching the photo. "I think something's…happened."

I take the poster from him. The revelation that Marnie used to work here makes me feel strange. Like, somehow, I'm filling her space, just taking over her job. I clear my throat and swallow hastily. "We'll put it up."

"You're sacked—both of you!" Mr. Richards shouts, pointing at me and then Lizzy.

Sacked? I stare at him.

Lizzy's mouth drops open.

The other customers are getting up and leaving now, in hurried movements, like they want to disappear as quickly as they can. I don't blame them.

"Get out, then!" Mr. Richards screams at me and Lizzy.

My hands are shaking as I place the teapot on the counter. I run to the staff room and grab my bag and coat. Lizzy is right behind me.

"Those are my aprons!" Mr. Richards shouts just as we're heading out the front door.

I turn to find him pointing a menacing finger at me.

"I'm not scared of you!"

"You should be!" he shouts back.

I practically rip the apron off, pulling a few strands of my hair with it, and shove it at him. Mr. Richards's nostrils flare even bigger.

Outside, the air is cool, and I take several breaths as I try to brace myself. Sacked? He's actually sacked us. I stare at Lizzy. She looks close to tears.

"I've got rent to pay," she whispers.

"I'm sorry," the man—Marnie Wathem's brother—says, and I jump and turn to find he's standing just to my right. "I didn't mean to get you sacked," he continues. "But that's got to be good grounds for a case of unfair dismissal."

I sigh. "You don't know the half of it."

"The half of it?" He's frowning, inclining his head toward me.

"He's a sexist pig," Lizzy says. "And racist."

"And ageist," I mutter. "Remember what he said when Collette wanted a job here?"

Lizzy nods. "Sexist, racist, ageist. And probably every other type of 'ist' you can imagine. We've been trying to collect evidence against him."

The man takes a step back. "My brother works for the Fair Work Commission. I can put you in contact with him. I'm Trevor, by the way." His eyes are sincere and bright as he looks at me.

"Jana," I say, and I find myself looking deeply into his eyes—because some eyes just make you do that. "And this is Lizzy. But I doubt we can do anything, we've only worked there a couple months."

Trevor raises his eyebrows. "Let's see what my brother says before we rule anything out."

"You really think we could get somewhere?"

He nods, surprisingly enthusiastic. "I can give my brother a call now, see if he's free tonight. He'll want to talk to you," he says, his eyes on me for a few seconds longer than feels necessary—but it also feels good. Like he's taking me seriously.

"Ah, I can't do anything tonight. Got to look after my niece and nephew tonight." I look to Lizzy. "You free?"

She shakes her head. “Studying to do.”

I look at Trevor. “Thank you—we’ll definitely arrange another time.”

He nods. “I hope so. And I’m sorry again.”

TWENTY-FOUR

Cara

"I HAVE HAD such a day, you won't even believe it," Jana tells me on the phone, the moment I answer, before I can even get a word in. Because I need to say how sorry I am to her, that I've taken Damien off her—because that's what I've done, isn't it?

And Jana sounds *angry*.

"Finally got sacked," she huffs.

"Sacked?" My voice is a gasp.

"Right! And I feel awful, because now Phia's there on her own. She had no idea when she went in for her shift that we'd not be there."

"What about Lizzy?" I stare at my bed cover. It's a floral design. Roses.

"She got the sack too!" Jana says. "It was crazy. But we've got this guy on our side. Marnie Wathem—you know, the missing girl?"

Of course I know of the missing girl. Well, *woman*. She's nineteen.

"We bumped into her brother, and he says he can connect me with their other brother who does something to do with unfair dismissals. I mean, Mr. Richards literally sacked me because I wanted to put up the missing poster for Marnie." Jana grunts. "Just ridiculous."

I sigh. I feel bad for Trevor. He's just doing what any brother would.

"So, what are you going to do now?" I ask Jana.

"Well, I'm watching the twins for the afternoon. Alicia's on shift again and there's like an hour or something before her boyfriend gets back, so I'm filling in there. And then I'm going to the cinema tonight," Jana says. "Me and Damien." She sounds happy, dreamy. "I can't believe he wanted to meet up again so soon. We only had that date on the moors yesterday."

It hits me like a punch to the stomach. I don't know why, but I'd assumed after my conversation with Damien yesterday, where I told him everything and we said we liked each other, that it would mean we'd be getting together—or something. That was what it sounded like, right? That's not me reading things into it... It can't be.

He blew me a kiss.

But he's still going to see Jana. He wants to see her? Keep seeing her? Or see us both? Unease fills me. Did he think I wouldn't find out? Or that she wouldn't? I grip the phone a little harder. Jana's talking excitedly about her date tonight with him.

For some reason, I thought tonight Damien would be messaging me tonight. He can't do that if he's with her.

Maybe he's not going to message me at all. I glance at the clock on the wall. He hasn't messaged me all day.

He's not going to.

He wants Jana.

Of course he does. He wants to be with someone who isn't afraid of the slightest touch. Was he just too afraid to say it to my face? He didn't want to upset me?

But of course he'd choose Jana over me.

Any person would.

Because I've got nothing going for me now.

I'm boring. I can barely work, some of the times I can barely walk, and realistically what would I offer someone? Why would someone want to be with me? Damian is better off with Jana, that's clear. He doesn't want to be walking round hospitals with me, waiting in overcrowded rooms with other patients ready to step into consultants' offices, queueing up at pharmacies to collect medication that only make it worse, or listening to degrading appointments where the doctors insist it's all in my head. What happens if Damian does accompany me to an appointment, one of the bad ones, where the doctors are patronizing and rude and tell me I am perfectly fine physically? Where they tell me about I want to be ill? Appointments I leave, shriveled up. What if Damian believes those doctors? What if he thinks it's all in my head, that I'm just crazy.

I know there's nothing wrong with it being in my head—I'm not against mental illness, but I'm against when it's used by doctors as an excuse to be mean that they don't know what is wrong and don't know how to treat you. Mental illness can't just be a diagnosis you also get when they don't know what's going on. That's harmful to those who are physically unwell with conditions such as Lyme disease, and to who to have genuine mental illness too.

Maybe I really am better off on my own. Single. Alone. Because there's no way I can try and date, not when I'm unwell. And even if I wasn't—what are the chances I would find someone who's ace or okay with me being ace? My mind goes to Rob and what he was like in the patio at the back of the club, and suddenly, I feel bad, dirty, contaminated. I blink and I see Rob in front of me.

I recoil.

"I hope you have fun on your date," I say to Jana, and I hope she doesn't hear the way my voice catches.

"Yeah, I can see why you liked him at the retreat," Jana says. I can tell she's smiling, happier than the start of this phone call. "He's just so nice, isn't he?"

"Yeah," I say. "He is."

I STARE BLANKLY at my graphics tablet. At the clean white screen. I should do something, draw something. I know it'll make me feel better. And I need to feel better. I shouldn't have thought about Rob again. Why did I? But I can't stop now. Can't stop imagining all sorts of things—and that makes me think of Marnie. What if Rob had been dangerous and hurt me and abducted me? What if I narrowly escaped abduction?

I take a deep breath. I need to calm down. I need to draw.

"Drawing is an expression of the soul," one of my lecturers at uni said once. She'd been standing at the front of the lecture theatre, wearing a long, flowing dress and a hideous neon-green shawl. She was one of those 'weird' lecturers. You know the type—the one who's a bit 'away with the fairies' and drinks herbal teas out of a flask they've made by hand, who only washes their hands with lavender soap they made themselves, and can never seem to remember quite what they're supposed to be doing. That was this lecturer. But her words stuck with me.

Drawing *is* an expression of the soul. Any art is. Raymond and I talked about this once, him telling me how making his computer animations is a way of connecting with himself again, of reminding him that he is more than just his Lyme disease.

But, as I stare at the blank white page on my tablet, I just feel empty. Like I have no soul. Maybe that's why I can't draw now—why I feel disconnected. Maybe the Lyme's finally reached my soul, and it's destroying me inside out, as well as consuming my body.

I want to draw something, but my fingers ache, and my head just doesn't feel right. I still don't feel right.

I set the tablet aside and stretch out on my bed. Maybe I should rest again.

And I feel a bit weird as I half-doze off, because I've rested a lot today, haven't I? But appointments are tiring, and they affect me for days. I know that.

I must've fallen asleep because suddenly it's dark. The darkness is a heavy fog over me and—

Something soft brushes against my face.

I jolt, fling myself upward, my hand flailing for my bedside lamp. I flick it on, heart pounding.

Something touched my face. Something touched my face. Something touched my face!

Fear rises in me, as I look around. What was it?

But there's nothing out of the ordinary. Nothing…

There!

I see it.

A cat. In the corner of my room, perched on the top of my bookcase. So high up. A freaking cat!

We don't have a cat.

Oh, God. It's the neighbor's cat. It's been outside and in other houses, and now it's in here, spreading the badness around and—

It's watching me. Its tail is hanging down over the top shelf, brushing against *Before I Go to Sleep* and *The Wife Between Us.*

My heart pounds. My books! My precious books! Being touched by a cat! A cat is in here, and, suddenly, I can feel the fleas crawling on it. It's infested! The fleas are getting on my books, crawling between the pages. And they're multiplying too, an army of fleas invading.

My breaths make squeaking sounds in my ears. My chest hurts. The side of my face it touched—must've been its fur as it jumped over me—feels like it's burning, like my flesh is corroding away.

How did this cat get in here? My window's locked—it always is. My bedroom door is pushed to—half an inch of light filters in from the hallway, all around the door. How did it push through?

The cat watches me, tilts its head to one side, then licks its lips in the exact way cats do on cat-food adverts. It's completely silent, and the hairs on the back of my neck rise as I stare at it.

I need to get it out.

But I'm frozen to the spot. I can't move. As soon as I move, the cat will move. It'll spring down from my bookcase, and it'll touch more stuff. It'll contaminate *everything.* Hell, its fleas are probably everywhere already.

My fear ratchets up a knot. My head pounds, and I struggle to breathe. I don't know what to do. I don't know what to do. I don't know what to do.

The cat's going to make a mess on my bookcase. What if it already has done? I try to scan around my room quickly, but without actually moving my head. Got to stay still. Can't move.

How long has it been in here? How long was I asleep?

But I can't see any cat mess. It's hidden it from me. The cat's being devious!

My nausea gets stronger. My teeth feel too cold. I look toward the door. Is Mum still downstairs?

I grab my phone and text her.

I need your help.

A few moments later, I hear Mum's footsteps on the stairs.

"Cara?" She calls softly through the door.

"Come in," I say, and my voice—it's not right. It's not me. It's someone who's crying. But then I realize I am crying. Tears are rolling down my face. "Come in *slowly.*" Can't startle the cat—the cat that's still watching me. It knows I'm scared. It's plotting how it can destroy my room. I can almost hear its thoughts.

Yes, I'll defecate on the bookcase, and then jump down onto the floor. I'll scratch behind my ear, sending my little flea minions across the room where they'll scurry for cover. Ha, ha, ha.

As Mum opens the door and steps in, I keep my eyes on the cat. Daren't look away. If it jumps, I need to know where it lands, which parts of my carpet I'll need to clean. Only it's probably walked *all* around my room already. And on my bed. My desk? My panic gets stronger.

"Shut the door," I whisper to my mum. The cat still hasn't moved.

Mum does so.

Slowly, I point to the cat. "Can you get it out?" I whisper.

Mum looks at the cat. "Get what out?"

"The cat!" My voice is a shrill shriek, so sudden it frightens me, doesn't seem to be part of me.

The cat hisses, but doesn't move, and my heart's pounding, and thank God it didn't move.

Sweat beads on my forehead, and I take a deep breath. "It's right there, Mum. Please. I need you to get it out."

Mum's giving me an odd look as she steps forward. She's taller than me, and she walks right up to the bookcase, until her face is level with the cat. The cat that's just sitting there.

Mum turns back to me. "Cara, there's nothing there."

"But it's there. I can see it!"

"I think you're hallucinating again," Mum says. "I think we need to contact your doctor."

Hallucinating. Just the word drives fear into me. I gulp, and then I'm crying more. "No, I'm fine. I'm fine!"

"It's okay," Mum says. "It's the brain inflammation. Dr. Singh did warn that it could worsen as we start to treat it aggressively, didn't he?"

Did he? I can't think.

I look back at the cat, and—

It's gone.

"Where did it go?" I yell. I jump up, standing on my bed, looking around. I need to find it. Have to find it.

"Cara, there's no cat here."

"There is—I need to get it out." My head pounds.

"Cara, I'm allergic to cats. I'd be sneezing if there was one in here. Come on," Mum says, holding out her hand, then she thinks better of it. I can't touch Mum at all—and I hate that I can't. Her comfort is what I need right now, but the OCD denies me that. "Come downstairs."

Yes, downstairs is safer. Downstairs there's no cat.

I leap onto the floor. Pain radiates from my left ankle, up to my knee, then my hip. Again, I look around for the cat.

I can't see it.

Hallucinations? No… It can't be. They haven't happened for a long time.

Tears fill my eyes, and I claw at my head, as if I can claw the badness out of my brain.

It's happening again.

TWENTY-FIVE

Jana

I RUN DOWN the street, nearly tripping in my heels. *Of course* I'm running late—I guess that's just who I am. I'm late for everything, it seems. And I'm still so far away from the cinema.

I curse loudly. I wasn't even busy earlier, thanks to being fired. I mean, Lizzy and I stayed talking to Trevor for a little while, but that was ten or fifteen minutes, maximum. And then I went to my sister's place to watch the twins who were both little devils as usual. But Alicia's boyfriend arrived after an hour, then I was free to go. My apartment was empty. River was at work. And I just…watched *Sex and the City* for the eighth time on my laptop, as I texted Damien. He didn't reply right away, and so when he did, my phone's ping made me jump. I'd asked him to go to the cinema with me tonight and he'd replied with 'okay.' Not exactly as enthusiastic as I'd hoped for, but people have bad days, I know that. Then I'd phoned Cara, and that was two hours ago, and I'm not really sure where the rest of the time went. Suddenly, I realized I was late and I got dressed up for the date super quickly, nearly twisting my ankle in the process as I jammed on my favorite pair of heels.

My heels now clatter on the pavement. It's been raining, and there are puddles everywhere, and I force myself to slow a little. Don't want to slip. That wouldn't be very attractive if I arrive at the cinema a crying, hurt mess.

I glance at my phone and groan. I swear time's speeding up, trying to make me even later.

I round the corner of the street and—

A hooded figure nearly crashes into me. I jolt back and—

It's Max. He sees me and grins. My mood darkens, and I try to step around him, but he stops me with a hand on my arm.

"Don't touch me," I hiss.

Max tries not to laugh as he removes his hand. I go to dart past him again, but now he holds his arms out wide, as if trying to block my way.

"Please, babe," he says. "I need another chance."

Annoyance fills me. "No, you don't. You really don't. Now, move, I'm going to be late."

"Late?" he squints at me. "Why you all dressed up like that?"

He looks me up and down—I'm in my favorite dress. It's short and black and revealing, and I know I have a great figure. I know I look killer. Black dress. Red heels, the exact same shade as my lipstick and purse that hangs from my shoulder on a fine, delicate chain.

"You're a liar," Max says.

"What?" I stare at him.

"You're not asexual—not when you're dressed like that, obviously on the pull."

"Hey." My voice is sharp. "I can dress how I want. That's none of your business and how I dress has nothing—absolutely *nothing*—to do with my sexuality."

"Why else would you have your tits out?"

I glare at him. "Because this is my favorite dress and dressing like this makes me feel confident. But I don't have to explain myself to you." I shove past him—and manage to dig my elbow right into him. He grunts.

Good.

"Whatever!" he yells after me. "Skank!"

By the time I get to the cinema, I'm fifteen minutes late, and on the verge of tears. Damien is leaning against the outside wall of the cinema, and he's looking strange—kind of blank of emotion. Not like how I've ever seen him before. But when he sees me, his face softens into concern.

"What happened?" he asks.

"Nothing," I mutter. I'm not going to give Max any more of my time or headspace. He doesn't deserve to have me speak about him. "Let's just get inside."

"Uh..." Damien starts to say.

A few raindrops fall on my face. "Ah, just my luck," I huff. "Rain! I haven't even got a coat. Is the universe just out to get me?" I shake my head, and, to my horror, tears are filling my eyes. And they're spilling over, down my face.

"Hey, what's the matter?" Damien's voice is still soft, but it sounds deeper now, stronger—like it can wrap around me and protect me.

"I lost my job," I say. "The boss from hell finally fired me."

"Oh, I'm sorry," Damien says, "but at least you can find somewhere better now?"

I snort. "Finding a job in this town is practically impossible."

Damien doesn't say anything, just stands there looking awkward—and no wonder, when his date has just turned up and started bawling her eyes out. There's no way he's going to kiss me now. And that just makes me want to cry more. I've ruined it. No way he's going to ask for another date after this. I wouldn't blame him.

"It'll be okay," he says.

"Let's just watch the film."

TWENTY-SIX

Damien

SHIT. SHIT. SHIT!

I was supposed to break up with Jana—but how could I? When she was upset? I'm not a heartless guy—I couldn't do that to her.

I groan as I sit down. My cup of tea's in front of me and I watch the steam billowing upward, but I suddenly don't want to drink it. I mean, it's late anyway. I should be going to bed. I just feel…bad. Like I'm stringing Jana along now. Oh, God. But that is what I'm doing—isn't it? Because I am interested in Cara. It's always been Cara.

But what if she is *too different now? What if you'd be better with Jana now?*

No. I can't think like that. I can't give up on Cara just because she's ill. I won't do that.

I stare at broken blinds above the kitchen window. The cord's all tangled together and the slats of the blinds are a mangled mess. I wonder how long it's been like that and why Cody's not fixed or replaced it. Does he never close the blinds in the kitchen?

The screen of my phone flashes. A text. Cara? Jana?

But it's neither of them—Jana's not texted since earlier, and Cara's not texted at all. Instead, the text is from Luke. A checking-in text. That's all. Huh. I bet Mum's put him up to it.

I'll reply later, tomorrow or something, when my stomach isn't churning over and over. When I've sorted out the mess that is my love life… But I don't even know how to break up with Jana—she's so lovely. It's not like when I broke up with my ex. I didn't like her by that point. I almost didn't mind that it would upset her. But I don't want to hurt Jana. I do like her—but only as a friend.

"Why is this such a mess?" I mutter.

"Because life is a mess."

Cody's voice makes me jump, and I spin in my chair to find him standing in the doorway.

"Man, how long have you been there?"

"Long enough to know you're having some sort of mid-life crisis."

"Mid-life? I'm *twenty-six*."

"Then get a grip of yourself," he says, all nonchalant, before he saunters away.

Wow. That guy's weird.

"Maybe I am having a quarter-life crisis," I tell Rufus as we walk along the woodland path the next day, the one Marnie took for that last walk, but of course Rufus is just a dog who doesn't actually care about anything I'm saying. All he probably cares about is whether Mrs. East has another roast dinner waiting for him when we get back. "It's all just such a mess, boy, you know?"

The path gets a little muddier and I slow my pace, trying to pick my way through it carefully. It rained a fair bit earlier and I should've put wellies on. It's not that I don't mind getting my trainers muddy, it's just that there are holes in them. And I hate getting mud on the insides of shoes. Makes them so hard to clean.

I extend Rufus's leash a little, giving him more slack. Not that he seems to want it. He's the least energetic of the dogs in my schedule. I've now got three other clients now, all of which contacted me this morning—two of which requested a group walk to socialize their puppies. But four dog-walking clients in total isn't enough.

"Guess it's not just my love life that's in tatters," I mutter, and of course thinking about my shoes makes me think of that ridiculous boring fact I produced at the retreat—and Cara.

Cara.

"She's going to think I'm not interested," I say to Rufus who, for the first time on this walk, shows the slightest bit of interest in something—rabbit droppings at the side of the path. "She's going to—"

There's a man coming toward me, walking another dog. A huge one this one, a Dalmatian.

I like Dalmatians as a rule. I mean, I like all dogs until the individual creatures give me reason not to. But I've always been especially fond of Dalmatians. No prizes for guessing which Disney film was my favorite back in the day.

Rufus, however, doesn't appear to like Dalmatians. Or at least not this one barreling straight for us.

"Easy," I say as Rufus lets out a low warning sound from the back of his throat.

His ears are alert and his hackles have risen. The Dalmatian's easily two or three times the size of Rufus, and dog fights can be nasty. Especially when one's athletic and one's overweight. I get ready to pick up Rufus, but he growls. Actually growls—and the dog runs right past us, but Rufus is still growling. The new dog seems…scared?

And Rufus growling at the Dalmatian's *owner*. A tall man with a wicked moustache and a dark trench coat. Big, army-style boots.

With a jolt I realize it's Mr. Richards. Jana's boss. That highly rude man.

Still, I give Mr. Richards a courteous nod as he nears.

He scowls at me. "You better keep better control of that mutt. Don't want him hurting my Buster. He's a pedigree, you know."

"That mutt?" I stare at him. "Just because this dog's not a pedigree like yours, doesn't mean yours is any better."

Mr. Richards glares at me, and Rufus's still growling, his hackles raised. I bet Mrs. East would be horrified to know how her precious boy is behaving right now. But I am proud of him. At least Rufus can sense what a horrible person this man is.

The Dalmatian makes a whining sound, and with a *hurumpf* sound, Mr. Richards continues on his way, albeit stepping rather heavily into a muddy puddle with his perfect boots, sending watery mud over my feet.

"Good riddance," I mutter, as he leaves.

Rufus watches Mr. Richards disappear down the trail and won't move until he's well out of sight.

"It's all right, boy," I say, but my heart's beating a little quicker now, and the air just feels heavier, like it's trying to sink me.

As we walk, I can't shake that feeling, and several times I become convinced that I'm being watched, followed, stalked.

But I'm not. Each time I turn, there's no one there. Mr. Richards and his dog are long-gone.

TWENTY-SEVEN

Cara

THE NEXT MORNING, I wake up and I can hardly see. Everything is fuzzy and green. The air has an almost iridescent quality to it. But I feel like sandpaper, like gravel is lining my eyeballs, each bit of each fragment of stone pressing in to be jelly of my eyeball. It's painful. And I can't see because there's a gray haze everywhere, a bit like a static you see on old TVs.

I take several deep breaths. *I'll be okay, I'll be okay, I'll be okay.* I repeat the mantra in my head.

I'm lying on the sofa, a blanket over me. I'm already contaminated thanks to the cat, two days ago—even the shower couldn't make it right—so lying on here still didn't feel too bad. And I couldn't go back to my room. Part of me is still convinced there's a cat there.

Last night, Mum left another voicemail message for Dr. Singh. He didn't seem to be working yesterday or the day before either. But he has to today, right? He'll be able to help me. I'll get help.

"Try phoning him," Mum tells me later in the morning, after I've eaten. "And remember to order your next prescription from him. You must run out soon."

I nod and get my phone out. The line rings and rings.

Then a woman answers. "Hello?" She sounds tired.

"Oh, I'm looking for Dr. Singh? He's my consultant."

The woman makes a sharp inhaling sound. "Oh, gosh, I'm sorry—I thought I'd already phoned all his patients . Dr. Singh was in a car accident at the weekend. He's currently in a coma."

What?

"Oh." My voice makes a squeaky sound after the word. I don't know what to say. I can't think of anything. My mind is blank.

"What's happening?" Mum asks me.

I put the phone onto loudspeaker, and then Mum and the woman are talking, the woman explaining to Mum what she just said to me.

"I'm terribly sorry to hear that," Mum says. "Will he be okay?"

Why didn't I ask that? Why didn't I say anything? I'm going to come across as a really bad person, like I don't care.

"We don't know what the prognosis is yet," the woman says. "More tests need to be done once he wakes up."

"Okay. Well, I'm sorry to ask this—but do you know what will happen to my daughter's treatment? Dr. Singh was treating her for Lyme and the resulting encephalitis."

"I'm afraid I cannot do anything. I'm not even a doctor, and he worked independently. I know there are other chronic Lyme doctors here too. I can email over their details. All I can suggest is that your daughter has her treatment and care managed by one of them. You should already have the test results, and I believe they can be transferred over to other clinics."

I feel sick. The words are swimming around me. Pain radiates behind my eyes, and I still can't see properly.

"Okay, thank you," Mum says.

I end the call and clench my phone back to me. Mum gives me a look and asks me something, but I can't understand her words.

I feel empty, void of emotion. Void of everything. And I know I shouldn't be making it all about me when Dr. Singh is in a coma, but I can't help feeling that this is where it all gets even worse.

"Two thousand pounds?" Dad exclaims.

We're sitting at the dinner table. I feel blank, empty. Mum and he are talking about the new doctor, one Mum phoned earlier. The doctor said that he can't continue my treatment without testing me for other things first. After Mum explained my symptoms and the return of the hallucinations, the new doctor—I can't even remember his name—said it sounded like I could have a Bartonella infection as well as Lyme. Apparently the two are common, and he said that his clinic uses different labs to what Dr. Singh did.

"They much prefer to run their own tests, and they are more detailed and extensive than the ones Cara's already had," Mum had told Dad. "If she's got Bartonella too, she'll need different antibiotics to the ones already prescribed by Dr. Singh."

"Then why didn't Dr. Singh test for it?"

"I don't know," Mum says. "But the new one mentioned something about a genetic test too." She looks at the notes in her hand. "Yes, for the MTHFR gene—he said he needs to know if Cara's got that, apparently she should already have been tested for that, as it could change the type of treatment she needs or something. But he's pretty certain that she's going to need IV antibiotics anyway. That oral ones aren't strong enough for her at this stage."

Dad makes a growling sound. "Dr. Singh thought they were fine."

"This new doctor has more experience," Mum says.

"And he won't just continue treating her on Dr. Singh's plan?"

"He said he couldn't, in good faith, do that. He's certain that other tests are required—and I don't think we can risk this. Cara's been unwell enough as it is."

They're talking like I'm not here, like I'm not at the table too, and it makes me feel weird. Then again, I can't really see them. Just the shapes of them, not the details.

"Sounds to me like he's just trying to get money," Dad grumbles. "He's twice the price of Dr. Singh. And, look, we've not got a lot left now. Those last tests wiped us out." He glances at me and then away again quickly.

"What choice do we have?" Mum says, her voice quiet, as if her volume has been turned down. Either that or she's running out of battery. "We need to get Cara better."

"Contact other doctors, too," Dad says. "There must be other private doctors. We need to find reviews of them as well." He turns toward me again. "Don't worry, Cara. We'll do something."

TWENTY-EIGHT

Cara

"I CAN'T BELIEVE we've only got three more days here," I say to Damien. He's sitting opposite me, the sun shining down on his now-tanned skin. It's amazing how quickly he's tanned. I haven't. I've just burnt. As usual.

"It's gone so quickly," Damien agrees.

He turns and watches a bird a few feet away. We're sitting on a patio area outside the hotel's main lounge. Everyone else on the retreat is in the pool—not too far away—and their excited shrieks reach our ears. I'd been about to go in as well, following Jana who was dressed in her brand-new bikini.

Damien had stopped me though. "Uh, do you want to sit with me?" He'd asked. "I—I'm not a fan of swimming."

I'd been wearing my swimming costume and had agreed to sit with him instead—of course I agreed!—and quickly changed back in my room into a loose T-shirt and shorts. And so we're sitting here now, the sun beating down on us, and it feels nice.

But three more days—that's all we have.

And I wonder what it'll be like after the retreat, what Damien and I will…become. Because we'll stay in touch, I'm sure. Of course we will.

I place my hands on the plastic table. It's not too hot. Damien smiles and places his hands on there too. Then he inches his hands closer to mine.

"I like your eyes," he says, staring at me with so much warmth and tenderness I immediately look away.

I can feel myself blushing. "Thanks."

The tips of his fingers brush mine.

"I like your eyes," I say back, and wow, it sounds kind of hollow, like I'm just repeating what he said. But I do like his eyes. Ever since the first day I saw him, I've liked the intense blue of his eyes.

Damien's fingers slide over mine. His touch is warm.

"I like you a lot, Cara. And it's crazy—I didn't think I'd find anyone I liked like this on this retreat. But I do like you. I just feel we're connected. You feel it too, right?"

I nod. Of course I do. "And I really like you."

TWENTY-NINE

Cara

A WEEK LATER, I take my last dose of antibiotics prescribed by Dr. Singh the Savior. It feels like a final moment. Like a line has been drawn in the sand and now I'm crossing it.

I'm going to be untreated again—and is it going to get worse? I mean, it's already got worse. I can hardly remember anything. Damien hasn't texted me—at least I don't think he has—so I'm certain he's chosen Jana over me. I haven't answered Raymond's calls because I just haven't had the energy. Haven't been able to draw because I can't concentrate.

In fact, I can't even remember what I've been doing. Other than reading—and even then it was hard to pay attention. Kept having to replay the chapter over and over.

I just feel so…lost. Like I'm floating in space, untethered, and no matter which direction I go, there'll never be anyone there who can save me.

With a jolt, I recognize what this feeling is. What it's the start of: the darkness. The monster.

I make my way into the kitchen. Esme's eating an egg sandwich and the smell of it nearly has me throwing up.

"You don't look good," Mum says.

"I don't feel it."

Mum purses her lips, doesn't say anything. I heard her and Dad talking yesterday. They only had enough money for three more months of prescriptions from Dr. Singh. And now that's not even enough for the first consultation—let alone tests—with the new doctor. I never fully appreciated just how affordable Dr. Singh's services were.

"Just rest," Mum says.

"I'll try."

I END UP talking to Jana. It makes me feel strange at first, because she got Damien and I didn't. But she's still my best friend. I know I do want her to be happy.

"I'm just not getting called for any interviews," she says down the phone. Her voice is a little staticky as the reception's not good. "It's like no one's even willing to give me longer than it takes for them to delete my application or whatever. Sorry—I shouldn't be complaining. You're the one with the real problems."

I hate my illness—my life—being described as a problem.

"It's fine," I say.

"No," she says. "Look, Damien and I were thinking about it all—"

"You talked to Damien about this?" My eyes widen. How much has she told him? Did Jana tell him I get hallucinations? Is that why he decided to stay with her rather than start something with me? Was that what tipped him over the edge, had him scurrying away from me, regretting that he'd ever spoken to me about our feelings and everything?

"Of course," Jana says. "He's really concerned. But, yeah, we wanted to get the okay from you on something. Like, fundraising—we thought we could get a group of us together and try and raise the money for you to see this new doctor. And you could set up a GoFundMe page too."

"I don't want everyone knowing," I say. "I'll just lose friends."

"Hey." Her voice is sharp. "You've not lost me."

"Yeah, but you know what River thinks about all this—and the more people I tell, the more people like her I'm going to encounter. There's already enough people being mean online." I think of the comments of how 'boring' I am.

Jana makes a considering noise. "But you do need this treatment. Damien and I have been looking into it more. The Bartonella stuff and the IV antibiotics. And this new doctor has a really great reputation. He's been able to nearly get rid of OCD via the IV treatment before. We've got to find some way to get you this help." She clears her throat. "We will."

"I can't tell everyone about it though," I say. "And if I set up a GoFundMe…it's just going to be awkward. Me asking for money."

"I can set it up," she says. "I'll do it for you, okay? We're going to get you better."

THIRTY

Jana

HELP MY FRIEND GET THE LIFE-SAVING TREATMENT SHE NEEDS – organized by Jana Hargreaves.

Hello everyone, my name is Jana, and I'm trying to raise money for my best friend, Cara. Three years ago, Cara caught Lyme disease after being bitten by a tick. The NHS treatment isn't sufficient, and they're unable to treat the brain inflammation that this has caused, so we're having to turn to private treatment. Obviously, this is very expensive—but it will be life-saving. Without it, Cara will likely get worse. She's already extremely ill from this.

Cara is an amazing person, and she really deserves this treatment. She's always been there for me, and now we need to be there for her.

If you can spare anything, we'd all be so grateful?

"Do you think that's okay?" I hand the laptop to Damien.

He reads it quietly, then he nods, handing it back to me.

I stare at the page, then click publish.

"How are you so nice?" he asks. He's sitting next to me at the kitchen table, and he looks uneasy. To be honest, I'm not even sure what is going on between us. This last week has been weird. We see each other and we talk and that—but we have yet to kiss.

I'm starting to wonder if it's going to happen at all. I mean, this morning when I answered the door, and he came in here, things just felt…weird?

"What?" I frown as I realize he's staring at me.

"You're just such a nice person," he says. "Like, doing all this for Cara."

"Of course. She's my best friend."

He nods, then runs a hand through his hair. He looks nervous.

"You okay?" I ask.

He nods again.

My phone pings. A message from Trevor. I'm meeting him later so he can get more details of mine and Lizzy's sudden dismissal from *The Red Panda*. He thinks we have some sort of case, especially when there's sexism—and racism, in Lizzy's case—involved and wants all the facts ready for his brother. But, again, we need proof, and now it's all down to Phia. She's still employed by Mr. Richards, and I hate seeing her go in to work on her own now. She said Mr. Richards hasn't hired anyone to replace me and Lizzy, somehow just expecting her to do all our work too. She hasn't even had a pay rise and she's expected to be there at all hours. He barely lets her have any breaks.

I read Trevor's message. It's the time and place we're meeting this afternoon.

"Um, Jana?"

I look up at Damien.

"Yeah?" I set my phone back on the table. He's frowning, looking sad and sincere. My heart jumps into my throat. "What is it?"

"It's…" He swallows visibly, his Adam's apple bobbing up and down. "It's you and me…*this*. We're friends, right?"

Friends?

"Well, yeah," I say.

He nods. "Because I don't think I can be more than friends with you—and I feel terrible, like I'm stringing you along."

For a second, everything goes numb. Just—everything. It's like I don't exist. Like I'm not here. Like there's nothing to me. I've disappeared, gone.

But then feeling floods back. A hot torrent shooting up both my legs, up my torso, to my head. My lungs seem to tighten, and my throat's too thick all of a sudden.

I swallow quickly and clear my throat. "Of course we're just friends." I laugh. "We're not together—I mean, we haven't even kissed!" My laugh gets louder. It's so obviously forced, and I can tell he knows it.

"I just… I'm sorry." He gets up. "I should go."

I don't stop him. I just stare after him as tears fill my eyes. I don't even try and stop them from spilling.

THIRTY-ONE

Cara

"HE BROKE UP with me," Jana gulps. She's standing in my hallway, shaking. Esme let her in, and the moment Jana was inside, she just seemed to melt. I've only seen her like this once before—crying, shaking, her fingers curling like claws so her knuckles get whiter. She wasn't like this when she broke up with Max. Just Ray—Ray who she really liked. "It's Friday the 13th, and he broke up with me."

So, she really liked Damien?

"I'm sorry," I whisper.

How much of a shitty friend am I that hearing that my best friend was dumped by Damien makes me happy? Because that has to mean he is interested in me, right? Unless he's not interested in either of us. I mean, he didn't break up with Jana right after talking with me. Left it over a week. Maybe he ruled me out right away, but has now realized he's not interested in Jana either. Not really.

I swallow hard, and I feel so awkward and useless standing here as my best friend cries. I can't even hug her. Can't even get close to her.

"I'm sorry," I say again.

"I should've known it wouldn't work," she says. "I mean…we didn't even kiss. I'd thought we were going to on the moors, but then he acted completely oblivious to it—and I thought he was being coy earlier this week, but now I don't think it occurred to him. Because he just wasn't into me, not really."

"Oh, no," I say. "But, Jana, you're an amazing person."

"Not amazing enough for him to want to keep seeing me." She tries to give me a smile, but just ends up crying harder.

"Come on," I say, indicating the living room with my hand. "Let's go in there. We can get ice cream, watch a film or something."

Jana nods and gulps, heading into the living room.

"I'll get the ice cream," I call after her, before rushing to the kitchen. I take several deep breaths. I can do this. I can sit in the living room. I can change my clothes later.

I grab a carton of ice cream. It's vanilla. The only type in our freezer. There's not much left in it, so I forgo bowls, just retrieving two spoons before heading into the living room.

Really, you're going to eat from the same carton as Jana?

The OCD is trying to scare me. It knows I can't eat much dairy or processed food anyway.

I take a deep breath, ignoring the OCD, and join Jana. "Do you want to put the TV on?" I ask. "Remote's over there."

Jana turns it on—I'm grateful I don't have to touch the remote—and she loads up Netflix on our Now TV box and selects *Enola Holmes.* "Heard this is supposed to be good," she says. "Milly Bobby Brown is in it. River wouldn't watch it with me because of that."

River the Repulsive. River the Rude. River the…Ratty?

As the film starts, Jana's tears lessen a bit, until twenty minutes in, she's completely engaged in the film. I, on the other hand, am not. It's always the same watching anything in here. I'm just on too high alert—now even more so than ever. Because what if I hallucinate again? The inevitability of it is a dark shadow hanging over me.

I pick at the ice cream with my spoon, careful always to scoop up a little from the opposite side to where Jana's getting hers from.

Jana leaves a couple of hours later, just minutes before Esme and Mum get back. They've been out at the library after Esme finished school, and food-shopping in town too, judging by the bags they bring back.

I relocate to my room and bring up another audiobook on my iPhone. I finished *Luckiest Girl Alive* a few days ago, but haven't selected a new title. I scroll through my audio library, then click one at random. *Stillhouse Lake* by Rachel Caine.

Just as I'm a couple chapters in, I get a text.

It's Damien.

I stare at the notification for a few moments, before opening it, uncertain of how I should feel. He really hurt my best friend.

But this is Damien texting me.

I click to read the text.

Can I see you?

Four words, so simple, so powerful. I stare at them, a thousand thoughts swirling through my head.

Okay, I reply. Because maybe this is it? Maybe this is the start of something? And I try not to think about what a bad friend to Jana this makes me.

I meet Damien outside High Court Flats, the same place where I met him on our date. He offered to come by my house, but I didn't want to risk it with Esme home. She could very well report to Jana.

Jana. I don't even know how I'm going to explain this to her. Because this is me and Damien getting together, isn't it? Not even a day after he broke up with her.

"Hi," Damien says.

"Hi." My voice is breathy. It's getting dark. I don't like being out in the evenings now. Especially after the night at the club.

"So, I… I'm not with Jana now," he says.

"I know." My voice sounds strange. My throat's a bit numb, and every part of my body is aching. The walk here was difficult, but I made myself do it.

"Because it's you I want." Damien gives me a grin. And he's expecting me to smile back? When my best friend's been dumped?

"She's really upset you know," I say. "Jana."

He exhales softly. "I—I don't know what to say." He looks up at the sky for a long moment. "I didn't mean to drag it out for so long with her. After we talked last time, I wanted to do it then, but…things happened. And it was… I just wanted to get it over with. I wanted to see you." There's hope in his eyes.

I nod. "I am pleased to see you," I say. "But…what is this?" I gesture at the space between us.

"This is us," he says. "This is what we should've done a long time ago. I can't believe how much has changed in three years."

"Do you think too much has?" I ask.

He shakes his head. "No. Definitely not. I just wish I'd been there for you, with all this, like, right from the start. We should've been coping with this together."

Together. I like the way that sounds.

He makes a sound deep in the back of his throat. "Cara, I'm not sure how to handle this—like, do you want to talk about your illness a lot? Or is it better if I don't mention it, like if we talk about other things? I just don't want you thinking that I'm not interested in your illness. I am. I just don't know how to navigate this."

This. Such a loaded word.

"I think I'd rather talk about something else, not focus on it," I say, and that feels right. I want to be myself around Damien, not the shadow that the Lyme has made me become.

Damien nods. "Of course." He gives me a smile that reminds me of all the smiles he gave me in Mallorca. I feel myself start to relax.

"We're going to have to be careful though," I say. "Jana can't know that we're…together." I almost trip up on saying the word—like I can't believe this is actually happening. "At least not right away. She's my best friend, Damien. I don't want to lose her."

"Of course not," he says. "And you won't. I mean, she has to understand, right? She was on that retreat too—she must've picked up on what was between us."

"She did." I smile a little. "She told me for weeks after to call you—and I kept saying I was too shy. I lost the book, you know. By the time I decided to be brave, I couldn't find it. Turned out, Esme had been sick over it and Mum had thrown it out. She told me a week or so later, said she'd buy me a new book." I'd felt raw when I'd realized that it had meant I'd have no way to contact Damien. "I did try looking for you on Facebook," I say. "Couldn't find you."

"Not on there." He gives a small smile.

"And I tried everything I could think of." I'm almost embarrassed to admit just how far I went—even getting the bus to Dorset one day, not realizing just how big the county is, and wandering around for a few hours, absolutely convinced that Fate would have me bump into Damien.

"But we're here now," he says, and I wonder what his reaction would be if he knew that I kind of went into stalker territory before.

The sky darkens more, and I look up at it. Looks like it's going to rain.

"Do you want to come inside?" Damien asks. "My apartment's on the second floor. And Cody, my roommate, is out. Got bowling club. Didn't even know that's a thing."

I look at the block behind him. Do I want to go inside? I'm already wearing my outdoor clothes, and I'm going to change when I get back. So, it'd be safe to, right?

I nod.

Damien's shoulders drop a little, and he looks more relaxed as I follow him into the building. We take the stairs, Damien asking me about the novel I'm reading—because of course he knows I'm reading one. So, then I start talking about *Stillhouse Lake*, and I just get carried away talking about the books I love.

"What?" I ask, when Damien looks at me with the cutest smile as we stop outside the door to his apartment. "I've been talking too much, haven't I?"

"You just seem more like you," he says, putting his key in the lock. "It's a good thing."

He opens the door, steps inside, and I follow him.

Air-freshener assaults my nose first. A lot of it. I nearly start coughing.

Damien's eyes widen and water. "Cody," he says. "He's always doing that. Says it'll smell damp if he doesn't. Not that there's any damp here anyway."

I follow him to the kitchen. He offers me a cup of tea, but I decline. I'm already on high alert, just being somewhere new. I need to take baby steps.

Damien makes his own cup of tea, then we head to the living room. After a moment's thought, I take my coat off and sit down, folding my coat carefully over my lap.

"You okay?" he asks.

I nod, smiling. "What's this?" I stare at the coffee table. It's covered in newspaper cuttings. *Everything* about Marnie Wathem's disappearance that's been in a newspaper seems to be on his table. Along with print-outs of articles and a school photo.

"Just a bit of background research ready," he says. "I am Damien the Detective, after all. And I never realized how much research a podcast episode takes."

The podcast. My heart does a little flip. "We're actually doing this podcast?"

"We told Trevor we were," he says. "And someone has to."

He smiles, but it doesn't quite reach his eyes now. There's sadness in them, I realize with a jolt, and I find myself leaning forward.

"What's wrong?"

"I just… I'm worried," he says. "Worried that Trevor is right and something *has* happened to Marnie. I mean, the gravity of it all is really sinking in. And if she is in danger, then she's only got us—amateurs—investigating." He shakes his head. "I'm just worried we're too late."

"Too late?" I stare at him, my mouth suddenly feeling too dry, kind of like sandpaper. "What do you mean?"

But I know what he means. Of course I do.

He locks eyes with me. "I've got such a bad feeling. You know I'm walking the same dogs she used to, right? Well, every time I go on that route, the one she last took, I feel like I'm doing something wrong."

"Like what?"

"Like I'm replacing her, just stepping into her shoes, like I'm a secret accomplice of whoever it was that wanted her gone. I know it's silly, thinking that, but I can't help it. It just makes it seem more real. Do you feel the weight of this all?" he asks. "Of us being the only ones looking into Marnie?"

"I haven't really thought about it," I say, and I feel bad, because I should've been. Because all along, this has been more of a fantasy to me, right? Something I'd do if I was healthy—save Marnie. I've never really stopped and thought about what would happen if Damien and I *did* discover that Marnie was in danger. If we did find proof. Because this isn't going to be like one of those made-up scenarios, where I was living in cloud cuckoo land, believing that I'd find her and save her and I wouldn't be held back by my Lyme.

Damien's right. This is serious. What if we do find something? And with the police not listening, would it be up to us to save her? To put ourselves in danger?

I swallow hard, feeling sick suddenly. I wouldn't be able to do anything heroic, I know that. Not when I'm ill like this. If I had to run from danger, my POTS would make me faint within seconds. And maybe the Lyme would stop me from running altogether in the first place.

Damien makes a half-shrugging motion. "Anyway, I was going to order pizza tonight. It's a bit early, but we could eat now."

"Pizza?" I say, and my heart's pounding. "Uh, sure."

Damien retrieves a couple of takeaway leaflets—both for pizza houses—and lets me choose. He places the leaflets next to me on the sofa, so I don't have to touch them, and once we've decided, he places the order, then sits next to me.

And it feels…. I don't know. Weird—especially with his research into Marnie on the table in front of us.

As we wait for the pizza, Damien asks me about the last few years. And of course, the only thing that's happened to me really in the last few years is my Lyme disease, so that's what we end up talking about.

The buzzer rings out, making me jump.

"Pizza's here." Damien jumps up and heads toward the door.

I stay seated on the sofa, staring at my coat that's folded perfectly over my lap. A blanket to protect me. And it is protecting me. With a jolt, I realize I've leant back fully into the sofa. My ponytail is touching the cushions—and probably the wall behind. And this is the first time I've realized it.

I think of what I'm like at home, sitting on the sofa. How rigid I am, how I'm constantly on high alert, how I try to lean forward so my hair and head and neck doesn't touch anything.

But here… here I can relax. I breathe deeply.

Damien returns with the pizzas.

I'm glad he ordered two separate pizzas. I struggle with sharing food, especially if another person's hands keep going in it.

"Have you got cutlery?" I ask.

"For pizza?" He laughs but then stops when he realizes I'm serious. Then he nods. "Sure." He disappears and returns a moment later with a knife and fork which he hands to me.

As I take them, my hand brushes his. An electric shock bolts through me.

We both freeze.

He looks at me, wide-eyed. "I'm so sorry."

"It was me." I stare at my hand, at my fingers looking exactly the same. Then I stare at the cutlery I'm now holding, and I'm trying to find imperfections on them, marks, because my OCD is making me look, and if I find anything my OCD will start screaming. And that's what it wants to do.

My heart pounds. I don't find any marks on the cutlery.

We settle down to eat, both on the sofa. Damien keeps a three-inch minimum gap between every part of our bodies at all times. But, as we eat, I find myself wondering what would happen if my leg did brush against his. Because nothing bad happened when my hand touched his. My OCD didn't start screaming like it would've if it was Jana or Esme or even my mum who did it. It's like…like the OCD's quiet. Like it's backed away, like it's sleeping.

And I stare at the smudge of grease that's somehow worked its way up the handle of my fork and onto the side of my thumb. And it's not bothering me at all. It's just there…and I haven't got an anxiety response to it.

Then I jolt a little. I'm sitting in an unfamiliar room, sitting on a sofa, and I'm not shaking.

I've been chatting happily with Damien.

Damien.

I look at him, and my breathing quickens—because it's him, and all my feelings that I felt on the retreat are flooding back.

It's *him*.

My heart pounds, and before I can change my mind, I reach across and place my hand on his.

Damien stares at me, his hand still in mine. "This is okay?"

My heart is pounding, and nerves are flying through me. The OCD's waking up—but maybe I can squash it down. And it's easier, because I know I'm going to shower later. If this was at my house, it would be a different matter.

But it's not.

I never realized it before—but my OCD can be quiet.

And when I test it, when I don't automatically shrink back at the slightest contact, following my usual routine, my OCD doesn't scream at me as much. Damien's here and I can touch his hand.

And oh my God—this is *that* stereotype, that chronic illness has a cure and it's a *man*. Shame fills me. It has to just be a coincidence, doesn't it? Or the distraction… But I can already feel the eye-rolls of feminists, as if someone they all know what I've just realized about myself.

I take a deep breath. Then I think of what Raymond said about Ali—how she seemed to lessen his OCD too.

"Yes," I say, holding his hand. "This is okay."

And it does feel okay—that's what I don't understand. I need to look this up. Because I've heard that romantic love causes neural changes in the brain. That the love hormones it releases can actually physically affect my brain. Could that be what's helping my OCD, is my romantic love for Damien reducing my brain inflammation?

Love.

I find myself smiling as I look into Damien's eyes.

THIRTY-TWO

Cara

"FOUR HUNDRED POUNDS already?" I stare at my mum in shock. She's got Jana's GoFundMe page open on her laptop on the kitchen table.

Four hundred pounds?

I just… I can't even process it.

Can't process a lot right now. Especially how yesterday I held hands with Damien—and I can't stop thinking about it. That physical contact did feel good. I hadn't realized how touch-deprived I've been thanks to the OCD. It's strange—I may have been able to overcome the OCD slightly with Damien, but back here it's on high alert. I moved so slowly past Mum earlier, afraid of accidentally brushing against her. And the same with Esme. It's like as soon as I'm in this house, my OCD's even more awake. And that just makes me feel bad—because I love Mum and Dad and Esme way more than Damien. It should be them that I'm comfortable around, not him. I can't explain it, unless the feelings I feel for him—the romantic ones—really are lighting up a different part of my brain that is just for romantic love and somehow that really *is* changing things and helping my brain inflammation. But what happens when my family realize I can touch Damien without panicking? I don't want to make them feel like I'm rejecting them.

"What time are you going to Jana's?" Mum asks.

"I'm not sure yet," I say. "Later."

Jana's just asked me if I can go over to hers this afternoon. She needs to enter my bank details into the Withdrawals section of the GoFundMe account so the money can be transferred to me. Just the thought of seeing Jana makes me feel bad. Like, somehow, she'll be able to tell that I'm now with Damien. That he broke up with her because of me. That she'll know that I've been holding hands with him—and it sounds silly, I know, but the look on her face when she realizes just sort of haunts me.

"I just can't believe Jana set this up," I say. "And people have donated four-hundred already."

"You can buy me a new tablet then," Esme shouts from the living room.

"This is for your sister's treatment," Mum says.

"I know," Esme shouts back, and I swear I can hear her rolling her eyes.

"Well, I can give you a lift to Jana's," Mum says. "If you want?"

I nod and breathe slowly, trying to quieten down the voices in my head, the fears. It's just a car-seat, I tell myself. I can change after—only I can't tell myself it'll be okay. And I don't know why the seats in Mum's car seem more dangerous than Damien's sofa. But they do.

"Maybe it's because you've tried for so long to keep your house a safe place," Raymond says when I ask him what he thinks about my OCD varying in intensity in different locations after lunch. "And so you're used to your OCD being worse when you're in the house. Or in your mum's car?" He pushes his hair back from his face. "I know with my OCD, a lot of it was just about habits, really. I'd got into the habit of doing things the OCD's way in my house, with my parents. I always found it so much easier to make progress outside of the house."

"But I just don't get it," I say. "I've never found it easy outside the house until now." Juist thinking what some of my hospital appointments have been like—where I've been terrified to sit in waiting rooms—almost has me shaking with the memories.

"Until *Damien*," Raymond says. "Look, you know Ali calms me. Maybe Damien calms you in the same way." He rubs his eyes. "There's got to be science in it, right? Like, is it endorphins? Or serotonin? You know, what your brain produces when you're with someone you really like. It makes you all calm and you don't care about anything."

It's exactly what I was thinking about yesterday.

I raise my eyebrows. "But I love my mum too," I whisper, and this has been going round and round in my head all day too. "But I still can't hug her."

"Not even like with a coat on?"

I shake my head, feeling like such a bad daughter. "Not even with a coat on." I sigh, thinking of how upset she and Dad and Esme will be if they knew I'd held Damien's hand. I can't even explain it, why it's different. Is it really because it's a different place? Because when I get home I'm washing all traces of Damien off me completely, putting all my clothes in the wash and jumping in the shower?

"Sounds like a question for your therapist," Raymond says with a chuckle. "But I'm proud of you, Cara. You've made progress. That's got to be a good thing."

I nod. Damien and I have arranged to see each other again tomorrow. And I've surprised myself by how much I'm looking forward to it. By how much my OCD isn't reacting. Maybe once I'm fine with him touching me, then I'll be fine with others too?

Just before five o'clock, I head out to Jana's apartment. It's been months since I've been there, and I sincerely hope that River's not there. I'm nervous as I walk from Mum's car, feeling sick and giddy, strange.

"You've left your lair then," River mutters, by way of a greeting when she opens the door. I'm just taking off my disposable glove, carefully folding it inside out. My finger feels burnt—I touched the doorbell, and I know logically there's nothing on my hand, not when I had the glove on, but I can't shake the feeling.

"Is Jana in?" I ask, bluntly ignoring her comment.

River gives a slight wave behind her with a flick of her hand. "Come on through."

Jana's in the living room, sitting on the blue sofa, her legs tucked under her, her Dell laptop on her lap. "You're here!" Her face lights up a little as she sees me. She clears space on the sofa next to her, rearranging the monstrous number of cushions so I can actually sit on the seat.

River settles down on the opposite sofa. "Don't suppose you're staying for girls' night?" Her tone clearly tells me I'm not invited.

"It's Saturday?" I frown. "Thought those were Tuesdays?"

"They are," Jana says. "This is an extra one. Phia needs the support—she's the only one working at *The Red Panda* now, and it's difficult. Plus, after my breakup I just want any excuse to see my girls. You can stay if you want, but no pressure, Cara. I don't know what time Phia and Lizzy are arriving, anyway."

"Won't it be past your bedtime?" River snorts.

I glare at her.

"Okay, yeah, here's the page," Jana says, twisting her laptop around a little so I can see the screen. I see her give a sharp look to River. "We've got to set up the withdrawals."

"Don't you feel bad?" River lifts one perfect leg and crosses it over the other. "Taking other people's money just so you can pursue this idea that you're ill?"

"You know what?" I stare at River. "I've had enough of you and your snide comments."

"Snide?" Jana mutters. "Hardly snide. She's blatantly direct about it. And being such a bitch, I might add."

River makes a huffing sound. "Look, I'm just being a friend here—"

"A friend?" I exclaim.

"Yeah, telling you what everyone else is thinking. Because you're obsessed with this idea that you're ill and you're even getting other people to pay for these appointments and things that you don't need."

My shoulders tighten, and I feel my bottom lip wobble. A tell-tale sign I'm going to cry. And that just makes me angry—because if I cry, I'm proving to River that I am weak.

"Hey, that's enough," Jana says.

"Oh, come on!" River rolls her eyes. "Look, Cara, babe, what you need is a shrink. You need therapy." She holds up her hands.

"I have *three*." I stare at her dryly.

"Cara is ill," Jana says.

"I actually have a disease."

"Yeah, one that's all in your head."

"*So what* if it was in her head?" Jana shoves the laptop to one side and stands up. "Is this how you'd treat me if I had a mental illness?"

"Nah, because I know *you* wouldn't behave like this." River laughs. "You've never been an attention-seeker."

"Neither has Cara," Jana says, her tone flat.

"Really?" River smirks. "Look at what she was like at school—always wanting to have your undivided attention, Jana. And, you, Cara, you never liked me because you knew I could see exactly what you are."

"I'm going to go," I say, standing up. My heart's pounding.

"No, you're not going anywhere," Jana says, and she holds out an arm in front of me, like she's physically trying to stop me from leaving. I recoil away from her arm. Jana turns on River. "*You're* going to go."

"Uh, what?" River looks outraged. "I live here."

"It's my mum's flat," Jana hisses. "And I can find a much better roommate than you."

River snorts. "Like her?" She shoots me a dagger-look. "Just you wait. Cara will have you being her nurse or something. God, why am I only the only one able to see her lies?"

"She's not lying." Jana's whole body shakes with each word. "River, pack your things. I want you out by this end of this evening. I've had enough. You're no friend of mine when you treat Cara like that."

It's weird sitting in Jana's kitchen without River giving me mocking looks. She stormed out moments after Jana told her to leave. Said she'd be back later once Jana had 'seen sense.' Meanwhile, Jana's packing River's things for her.

"I can't believe how much shit she has," Jana shouts from River's room.

"Yeah," I say, and I sound pathetic. But my heart's still pounding from the confrontation, and I feel sick. "Do you think she actually will leave? Like, won't she do something to stop you?"

"Like what? Girl, she's going. I'm telling you."

The sounds of bags rustling fills the flat and then Jana appears in the kitchen, dumping two bin-liners of clothes on the kitchen floor.

"That'll do for now."

"Thanks," I say.

"What for?"

"For sticking up for me," I say. "For being my friend."

"Girl, I'm always your friend."

“Thank you,” I say, and I try to pretend that my gut isn’t squeezing because I’m a bad friend. Because I’ve taken Damien from Jana and she doesn’t even realize it.

THIRTY-THREE

Cara

"I CAN'T BELIEVE we both found people!" Jana grins at me as we're packing our suitcases. "You and Damien, and me and Ray!"

Ray gives her a cheery wave from the other side of the hall. He's not the type of guy I'd have put Jana with. Usually, she goes for really tall and muscular guys that have the typical 'bad boy' vibe: you know the kind, has floppy blond hair, is usually in a band, has a minor drug problem that Jana believes she can fix. But Ray's different: he's four inches shorter than her, two years younger, skinny as a rake, and has what Jana said a week ago was a 'cute, nerdy look.' He's really into video games and his screensaver on his phone is a flamingo.

"So, you two are meeting up back home?" I ask Jana, giving Ray a quick nod.

"I think so—like, it just feels, right, you know?" Jana is practically bubbling.

I think of Damien, and I do know.

"We were talking a lot last night," Jana continues. "And Ray and I think…we think we can make this work. We're both gray-ace, so that's a relief."

"Isn't he aro?" I ask. "Like, how will that work? You're into romance."

Jana nods. "But that's what we were talking about—like, the whole relationship thing. He doesn't like fall in love romantically, only platonically. He still likes kissing though, but he doesn't see that as romantic, that's more sexual for him. But he still wants to have that one special person. And, sexually, we're good." She gives me a knowing look.

I lean in closer. "You've slept together?"

"Don't look so scandalized!" She laughs and tosses her hair back. "Plenty of aces have sex."

I nod. "Yeah, I didn't mean otherwise…" I trail off as David and some of the others enter the room.

David is glaring at me, and I try to ignore it. Try to tune fully into whatever it is that Jana's now saying. But I can't. It's like his gaze is burning me and Jana's words just float away. He's been against me ever since Damien and I won that chocolate.

"What?" I ask David, finally, the moment Jana's stopped talking and has gone over to speak to Ray again.

David looks me up and down. "You think you're so perfect, don't you?"

"Uh, what?"

"Just because you found Damien here."

"I never said I was perfect," I say.

"But it's not love, and it won't last." He points a finger at me. "He's only been pairing up with you because this retreat it encourages it. But you're boring, Cara, and out in the real world he wouldn't look twice at you."

I feel like I've been punched in the gut. My mouth dries, and I stare at him, try to think of something to say. Try to…

But I can't.

He smirks. "Must hurry. We're leaving soon." Then he leans in closer. "Smile, darling. You don't look anywhere near as cute when you're frowning like that."

I swallow hard, turning away from him. My fingers fidget at the zip of my hoody. David's wrong—completely wrong. Damien likes me, and he's not just with me because the retreat pressures people into couples. I mean, if that was the case then everyone here would've paired off. But they haven't. It's just me and Damien, and Jana and Ray. Though I did see Freda and Bianca getting cozy too.

But still, David's words have sunk into me, and I can't shake them. When Jana returns, I mention it to her, trying to sound all casual and not affected at all by David, but Jana's my best friend and she sees through my bravado instantly.

"Ignore him," Jana says. "He's just jealous. Remember what he said in his introductions? How he was going to find 'the one' here? And of course he's a dick, so no one's interested in him like that. So, he's just trying to ruin your happiness because he's jealous."

"But what if he's right? What if Damien isn't interested in me outside of this retreat?"

Jana rolls her eyes. "You know he is, girl. You—"

"Phones!" Mrs. Mitchell's voice booms out, and I jump, find her standing in the middle of the lobby with a wide grin. "Come and get your phones."

There's a flurry of movement as people gravitate toward her. Practically everyone else is here too now, and I search for Damien. Just seeing his smile will reassure me, I know that.

There he is. I spot him at the back of the room, and I wait until he's going to get his phone from Mrs. Mitchell before I approach for mine too.

"And these two are the last ones left," Mrs. Mitchell says, smiling even brighter. "Let's hope they're your phones else someone's thought they'd do a swap!"

All around us, everyone's powering their phones on. Two weeks without phones has been strange, but I know I found it easier than others.

"Swap numbers?" Damien's voice is low and rich, and he's so close to me I can feel his breath on my face. He smiles, but I'm searching his face now for insincerity. What if David's right and Damien's not interested in me? But he is asking for my number…but what if that's just because he feels like he has to?

He might never reply to my texts.

"Sure," I say, and my voice wobbles, and I'm telling myself not to be worried. If David hadn't said anything, I'd not be thinking about this at all.

Damn. My phone won't turn on. I grab my charger from my rucksack and plug it in, but it doesn't do anything.

"Is it broken?" Damien's squinting at my phone, and he looks worried.

"Probably just the charger," I mumble. "Not the best one." Or at least I really hope it's the charger. I can't afford to get a new phone.

"Well, I'll take your number then," Damien says.

"Uh…" I look at him. "I don't know it. It's a new SIM card, one I only got a week or so before flying out here. I hadn't learnt the number yet."

He looks momentarily surprised. "Well, let me write my number down for you," he says. "Got any paper?"

I search through my bag, my heart pounding. It's too hot in here, and my fingers are sweating. The only thing in my bag that contains paper is the book I'm reading. Gone Girl *by Gillian Flynn.*

"I've got a pencil," Damien says, nodding to the book. "Hold on."

I wait for him to produce the pencil from his own bag, and then he's writing his phone number on the inside of the cover.

"Now you won't lose it," he says with a smile as he hands the book back to me.

"Great," I say, and I try to quieten my pounding heart.

THIRTY-FOUR

Jana

"I STILL CAN'T believe you threw her out yesterday." Lizzy stares at me with wide eyes. "River's gonna be so mad."

"Yeah well," I say. "Someone had to do something." I shiver a little and pull my jacket around my shoulders. It's getting colder now, feels more like autumn. I watch several amber leaves as they dance through the air on their way down.

Lizzy makes a disbelieving sound as she leans against the tree trunk. "Still, she's gonna be *mad*."

I try to put River and her anger out of my head. Lizzy and I aren't here for that. We're here to meet Trevor. He's spoken to his brother about our case, and asked if we could meet him.

"And where's she even gonna live now?" Lizzy asks. "She hasn't got family here now."

"That's not my problem," I say.

"Really?" Lizzy raises her eyebrows. "She's still your friend, Jana. She's still—"

"Ah, look, there he is," I say, grateful that I can see Trevor hurrying along. He's dressed casually today, and I find myself admiring the way his jeans cling low to his hips.

The faintest stirrings of *something* awaken within me, the lightest bits of interest in him—sexual attraction—but then it disappears.

"Hello, sorry I'm late." Trevor nods at each of us. "Shall we go and grab a coffee? Not from *The Red Panda*." He laughs, but I can tell it's forced.

My mouth dries a little. "Sure." I say.

As the three of us walk into town, I can tell it's bad news. Trevor would've been smiling or something by now if he had good news. Not walking quickly, hands in the kangaroo-pouch pocket of his hoody.

We take seats in the café on Main Street. It's Sunday, and it's only open for an hour more today.

"I'll get these," Trevor says, as Lizzy and I both order a mocha. I wince—another sign it's bad news.

"Just get it over with," I say. "We haven't got a case, have we?"

Trevor exhales for a long moment, and as soon as the waitress has moved away, he turns soulful eyes on us. I hadn't realized before just how expressive his eyes are, but now they hold no secrets.

"I'm sorry," he says. "Paul's said it'd cost you more in legal fees if you try and do anything than if you just let it slide."

"Even though he sacked us unfairly?" Lizzy asks. "Like, we did *nothing*."

"You've only been working there a few months," he says. "That works against you in cases such as this. And there's little evidence—I mean, I know I was there and saw him fire you—but I mean even then it'll be my word against his. And he'd probably try and drag up all other reasons to justify his decision."

I let out a low growl of frustration.

"Sorry it's not better news," Trevor says, and he looks genuinely disappointed.

"It's okay. Not your fault." I try to give him a smile, but my heart's just not in it.

"I'm still sorry."

Lizzy and I end up buying a basketful of ice cream—it was on offer at Co-Op—and we head back to mine. River has indeed cleared all her stuff out, and it's amazing how empty my apartment is without her stuff. Her ornate lamp. Her books on the bookshelf. Her elephant ornaments on the fake mantelpiece.

"Phia should be here soon," I say, glancing at my watch as we spread out the ice cream cartons on the coffee table. And sure enough, no sooner have I said the words, when the doorbell rings. Phia texted me earlier to say she'd be calling around after finishing work. Mr. Richards is trying to keep *The Red Panda* open on a Sunday for as long as possible.

"I'll let her in," Lizzy says. She's already halfway to the front door.

I peel back the lid of the salted caramel ice cream and dip my spoon in—and hear Phia crying.

"What's the matter?" Lizzy's voice is high-pitched.

Holding my ice cream, I run into the hall. Phia's still in her waitress uniform, complete with the apron that Mr. Richards is very particular about not leaving his premises, and tears are streaking her winged eyeliner down her cheeks. Lizzy pulls her into a hug.

It takes several moments for Phia to calm down enough to tell us why she's upset. And, when she does, my blood boils.

"He did *what*?" I stare at Phia, my hand frozen in mid-air. The spoon in my grip slackens, and the glob of ice cream on it nearly falls. I shove the spoon back in the carton and turn my whole body toward Phia.

"I don't think he meant to," Phia says quickly. She shakes her head, then looks down at her hands. She's laced her fingers together. "I mean, he probably just slipped or something."

"Slipped and his hands landed on your chest?" I snort.

"Don't defend him," Lizzy says. "That's sexual harassment. You need to report him."

Phia's shoulders drop a little. "But he'll know it was me reporting him—given I'm the only waitress now. And then he could be worse in the next shift."

"Uh, girl, you ain't going back there."

"Jana's right," Lizzy says. "You can't. He's a creep."

I swallow hard, feeling sick. We never should have left Phia on her own after Lizzy and I were sacked. We should've persuaded her to quit or something. "Have you reported it to the police?"

"The police?" Phia looks shocked. "No."

"Well, you need to. He can't get away with this."

Phia's eyes water. "It'll just make things worse. And, anyway, what good will getting the police involved actually do? They're not going to believe *me*." She shakes her head. "No, no police."

"Let me call Trevor then."

"Trevor?" Phia frowns at me. "How is he going to help?"

"His brother was helping me and Liz." No point telling Phia that that case was pretty much closed though.

"Yeah, with *unfair dismissal*," Lizzy says. "Not sexual harassment."

"But we told them Mr. Richards's is sexist and racist. And now this." I look at them, and when none of them try to stop me, I call Trevor.

He doesn't answer.

I fire off a quick text to him instead.

"I can't believe this," Lizzy says. She looks closely at Phia who's looking decidedly green. "Are you okay?"

Phia nods. "I just want to forget it happened. Come on, can we watch a DVD or something?"

THIRTY-FIVE

Damien

"OKAY? CAN YOU hear me?" I peer at my laptop screen, at the little square where Cara's face is. I bought a subscription to Squadcast yesterday, and today, Cara and I are trying it out. She's logged in at her house and I've invited her as a 'guest' onto the podcast.

We're really going ahead with the *Damien the Detective* podcast, and there's something so exciting about doing this with her.

Today is just a test though as we're both getting used to using Squadcast.

"Yep, I can hear you," she says. She leans closer to her camera, and even across the interwebs, I can see the brightness in her eyes. "So, who do we plan to ask to be guests?"

I look down at my notebook. It's on the table next to my laptop. "Obviously Trevor," I say. "I messaged him yesterday, and I also asked about their parents or the other siblings. I told him usually podcasts try to interview the people around a missing person, you know, to really give a sense of who they are."

Cara nods. "Does he think they'll agree?"

"He's not sure. He is the only one who thinks she's actually missing. So, there's that. But you and Marnie had some of the same teachers, right?"

"Must've. Though there was a high turnover of staff at the school though."

"But you'll know some of them," I say. "So ,can you message them? See if any of them are up for it? I also want to talk to the cops if I can. I mean, it's going to be difficult, but we need this to be as close to a professional podcast as we can, and those always include talks with detectives."

"And clips of the calls made to the police by the family or whoever reported them missing. That was Trevor, right?" Cara says. "There must be a recording of the call he made to the cops about her not coming home."

"Oh, there will be. Just depends on whether we can actually get access to it. Pity we haven't got someone like Marnie with us who's into computer science."

Cara nods, but then stops.

"What?"

"I do know someone. River Charles. Uh, she's friends with Jana. Well, used to be friends with her. And with me too…" Her voice has gone flat.

"What is it?" I ask.

Cara looks down. The screen flickers. "Uh, she's been quite mean to me. About me being ill. And it sounds stupid. I'm twenty-five, I shouldn't let this affect me. But she's been spreading stuff about me."

I lean forward, my heart beating quicker. "What kind of stuff?"

Cara shrugs a little. "Just saying that I'm faking being ill. About a month ago, she and some others kept tagging me in stuff on Facebook. Stuff that implied I was making it all up. You know, things about people playing the benefits system, stuff like that. They were quite mean. Said I was just a boring sick girl who wasn't actually physically sick. Just sick in the head to want to trick people."

My breath freezes in my throat. "What? That's… oh, God. Cara, that's horrible. I'm so sorry." I frown. "And Jana's still friends with this person?"

Cara clasps her hands together. "Well, until the other day. It was amazing really. Like, River had a go at me. I was at Jana's place, and River had a go at me, but Jana just kicked off. I've never heard her do that before—but she threw River out."

"Wow." I blink. I can totally imagine Jana doing that though. That woman's fiery. But then I feel bad for the way I treated her—because I did lead her on, didn't I? "Well, we won't ask River for technical help," I say, wanting to move the focus away from Jana. "I mean, maybe the police will release the call to us?"

"Maybe." Cara shrugs.

"Anyway, shall we run through the script?" I ask. It's a practice script, one I wrote last night. A rough kind of introductory piece.

Cara nods. "Sure. It won't take long, will it? I need to get to Boots to pick up my NHS prescription."

"That's fine," I say. "And I can meet you there, if you want?"

"Uh, yeah, okay. But I'm not feeling that well so I don't know if I'll be up for anything."

“It’s okay,” I say. “I just want to see you. That’s all. I can walk you back home.”

She smiles, and it’s the kind of smile that eats me up inside. “Let’s get on with this podcast then.”

THIRTY-SIX

Jana

I STARE AROUND my empty living room. River has taken the sofas. The men—no idea who they actually were—only left a few minutes ago, carrying the sofas between them. Four strapping guys. They said River had sent them to pick up the rest of her stuff.

I perch on the windowsill. The apartment looks even emptier now. I breathe out a sigh. Empty and lonely and quiet.

Then my phone buzzes.

Would you like to go for a coffee this afternoon?

I stare at the text from Trevor.

Have you got news? I write back.

There's a pause in which the three floating dots appear on my screen. He's typing.

No. I meant just…a coffee with me.

A coffee with Trevor Wathem? My heart suddenly pounds a little. Like…a date? He's asking me out?

And it would mean I'd be getting out of this empty, quiet apartment. I mean, I've got to go into town anyway. I've still got a key to *The Red Panda,* and Mr. Richards left a rather rude message on my phone last night, demanding I return it or he'll report me for theft. Huh. I'd love to see him try.

I'd been dreading going into town, just to return the key, but now I have a reason to go that doesn't center my whole life around Mr. Richards.

Sure, I reply to Trevor. *I'd love to.*

"So, you have no seats in your house now?" Trevor's staring at me.

I tried to tell it as a funny story, but I'm not really sure the humor's come across.

"No," I say. "None. I mean…she didn't even pay for them. They were free to a good home. That's what the Facebook Marketplace advert said. *Free*. And now she's taken them!" I force out a laugh, and my hand on my coffee cup jolts with the sound—like I didn't actually expect to laugh so loudly and the rest of my body wasn't ready.

"Wow," Trevor says. He takes another sip of his mocha. "Just…wow." He gives me a smile—a deep smile that transforms his whole face.

And, suddenly, it hits me just how conventionally attractive he is. Bright, big eyes. Long lashes—the kind that make me a bit envious. Killer cheekbones—as in a seriously good facial structure. A square jaw with a few-days'-old stubble. He's tall too—and I like tall men. Especially tall men that talk to me like I'm a real human being.

I find myself smiling back at him. I shift a bit in my seat. The key to *The Red Panda* digs into my pocket. I'm not looking forward to seeing Mr. Richards's smarmy face when I drop it off later.

"Don't suppose you know of any jobs going?" I ask, and I don't know why I suddenly want to talk about work—or, rather, my lack of it.

"My firm's hiring," he says.

"Your firm?" My eyebrows shoot up, and I don't know what Trevor actually does, but suddenly I'm imagining working alongside him, having more opportunities to talk to him. To get to know him. Because, I realize with a jolt, I do want to.

"Yeah. I work in operations management."

"Which is?" I blink.

"We help businesses with the logistics of running operations."

I nearly laugh. "I still don't really know what that is."

"We work with other companies, helping them manage their productions operations. We've got a quite a few clients. Lots of banks actually."

"Ah, okay," I say.

He laughs. "You've still got no idea what I do, have you?"

I give him what I hope is an endearing and cute grin. "Nope!"

I look at Trevor, across the table, and I think I could like him. Like him, properly. I mean, he looks good, that's for sure. And I know he's a decent bloke. A really decent bloke, who I'm currently on a date with.

"Looks like they're closing up here," Trevor says.

I turn and see the waiter is wiping over the tables behind us. We're the only ones in here now.

"Fancy a walk?" I ask. "Just 'round the park?"

"Definitely." He smiles widely.

We leave a tip and head out. Trevor talks now about the rabbit he had as a boy—I'm not entirely sure how the subject came up.

"No way he was called Thumper!" I exclaim. "That's what mine was called!"

He fakes being positively shocked. "What are the chances?"

"Yeah, not like it's a common name for a rabbit!" I laugh.

We wait for the traffic to slow and then cross the road.

As we walk, I look down and twist my ring. It's a black band on the middle finger of my right hand.

"Oh, is that an ace ring?" Trevor asks suddenly.

I jolt. "You know about the ace spectrum?"

"Oh. Uh, yeah." He nods. "I was in the LGBT society at uni."

"You were?"

He nods. "I'm bi."

"Oh," I say as we reach the gates for the park. "I'm ace. Gray-ace, to be precise."

"Gray-ace?"

"In between ace and allo—uh, straight," I add. Because I always forget that the average straight person doesn't know what 'allo' means.

"Okay," he says. "Cool."

"Cool?" I stare at him.

"Yeah," he says. "I mean, look, I like you, Jana. And this is only a date, right? Not like we're getting married or anything now." He laughs. "Anyway, you can tell me more about what being…gray-ace…" He looks at me for confirmation, and I nod. "You can tell me more what it means for you, make sure I understand."

A warm feeling fills me, and I smile, find myself stopping, leaning in closer to him. He stops too, and then we're inches apart. My hands find their way to his waist, and I hold onto him. His hands go to my shoulders, his fingers lightly kneading my skin.

He smiles.

"Well, being ace is... I don't know how to describe it," I say, staring up into his eyes. He really has beautiful eyes. "I just... It's just normal for me, and everyone sort of expects me to spout out this huge speech. But I never have a huge speech. It's just me. And I just, I like sex. Let's get the awkward part of the conversation out of the way, right?"

He laughs.

"So, yeah, I like sex—and being ace doesn't mean we never have sex. Some do. Some don't. Being ace is about whether you feel sexual attraction, not whether you actually do it. And yeah, I feel it. Sometimes. Often it's low. But I don't know." I laugh.

"So, do you like kissing?" Trevor's voice is low, teasing.

I smile as I look up at him. "Well, maybe we'd better find out."

I stretch onto my tiptoes and—

My ringtone blares. Trevor and I spring apart. My heart pounds, and I pull out my phone, looking at the screen.

Phia's mum, Mrs. Byeon, is phoning me.

I stare at the screen for a moment, frowning. Mrs. Byeon has never phoned me before. I only have her number in case of an emergency as Phia's allergic to beestings and asked me to have her mother's contact just in case.

I click to accept the call. "Hello—"

"Is Sophia with you?" Mrs. Byeon asks, speaking over me.

"Uh, no. She's not," I say. "Why?"

Trevor's giving me a questioning look, but I turn away from him.

"She's not answering her phone," Mrs. Byeon says. "And she should've been back from work hours ago. It's her sister's birthday, and Sophia said she wouldn't be late."

"Wait, she went to *work*?" I nearly choke. Phia promised she wasn't going to go into work. Not after Mr. Richards touched her inappropriately. My head pounds.

"I was not happy about it," Mrs. Byeon says. "But she said her boss called her and said he was short-staffed. She told me she was being paid double and it would just be an hour this morning, that's what she said, that she would definitely be back in time for Taryn's party."

The whole world seems to stop. I go to take a breath, but the air's stopped too, and nothing fills my lungs. They're just empty.

For a second, I can't speak. Then feeling fills me like water breaking through a flimsy dam.

"Call the police." My voice wobbles. My breaths come in short, sharp bursts. Hell, what if I'm over-reacting? But what if I'm not?

"The police? She's only a few hours late," her mother says. Then her tone changes.

"Just..." I blink rapidly. Am I over-reacting? Then I look at Trevor. Marnie's missing, and she worked for Mr. Richards too. My stomach twists.

"Jana, what do you know?" Mrs. Byeon asks.

Ice fills my veins. "Did she tell you what our boss is like?"

Judging by the long pause, I guess not. But I can't go into it all now. I just can't. Something tells me I'll need my energy.

"I'll call the cops," I say before hanging up. I'm breathing too fast, and I feel all jittery.

"What's going on?" Trevor asks, but I'm already typing in the emergency number.

"Phia's missing," I pant, suddenly out of breath. The world seems to spin. "And Mr. Richards… He touched her chest the other day, and she was upset, and—"

"He did *what*?" Trevor looks at me, his face frozen in panic.

"I think it was *him*—look, Marnie worked for him too, right?" I feel sick. "And now Mrs. Byeon said Phia was working today—even though she told me she wouldn't go back there—but she's not come home, and Phia would never miss her sister's party. And with Marnie working for him before and… It *has* to be him, right?"

Trevor's eyes widen. "Have you tried phoning Phia?"

I touch my forehead. My fingers are cool against my sweaty skin. "No… I'll do that now then."

I feel sick as I delete the emergency number and instead select Phia's contact. I hold my breath, begging her to answer as the line rings and rings.

"Nothing," I say to Trevor. "It's him, right?"

But what if her phone's just out of battery? What if I waste police time?

But what if Phia's in trouble? What if he took Marnie too?

Trevor's voice is dark when he speaks. "We can't take risks." He nods, and his eyes narrow a bit. "Let's go."

"The café?" I stare at him. "I've got my key still."

"No, his house. I can get his address."

"But Phia could be at the café," I say, and I know I'm just hoping. "We're right by the café."

"Fine. But if she's not there, we go to his house. Call the police on the way. We can't waste time." His voice is strained, and I know he's hoping that we find Marnie too.

I nod, breathless, and then we're running, and I'm phoning the cops.

"Yes, we think our friend's been abducted," I say, but I'm wheezing. My asthma.

Trevor holds out his hand for the phone.

I nod, hand it to him. My heart pounds.

"Yes, her name is Phia…" Trevor looks at me. "What's her full name?"

"Sophia Byeon."

"Yes, Sophia Byeon. And we think her boss—Mr. Richards at *The Red Panda,* it's a café, we think he has taken her. He's who Marnie Wathem used to work for too, and she's missing too—despite what those detectives say…"

I struggle to breathe as Trevor speaks. My heart pounds. It seems to take an age to get to the part of the town where the shops are. It's a countdown. And I also don't know if we'll have to go to Mr. Richards's house. Or where he lives.

Trevor and I speed up into a run, and he's still talking to the police, panting out words, and—

Damien and Cara—they're here? Walking by the café. Cara's holding a Boots bag and Damien's laughing as she says something.

My heart quickens. Are they… I inhale sharply as I see the way he's looking at her. My stomach feels a little heavier.

"Why are you slowing?" Trevor barks at me. He's still got my phone clamped to his ear.

I point at them. "My friends—safety in numbers!" And then I'm running.

Horror crosses Damien's face when he sees me barreling toward him, and then Cara's looking worried.

"Need your help!" I shout. "Phia's in danger!"

THIRTY-SEVEN

Cara

"WHAT?" MY HEART pounds as I stare at Jana and Trevor. Phia's in danger? I rush forward. Damien's right behind me.

"It's Mr. Richards," Jana shouts. "He's taken her, I'm sure of it."

"He could have Marnie too," Trevor yells.

Marnie? My heart does a jumpy thing.

Jana's breathless. "Come on."

The four of us practically fly the remaining distance to the café, and, somehow, I'm running without my body threatening to give out. It's the adrenaline, it has to be. My Boots bag bangs against my thigh.

The Red Panda's in darkness.

Jana grabs the door handles and shakes them. Locked. She digs a key out of her pocket and jams it into the lock. The door opens moments later, and she practically falls in.

"Phia!" Jana yells, and then Trevor's inside too and Damien. I hurriedly follow, trying not to brush against everything.

"You okay?" Damien asks, his voice low.

I nod, but everything feels like it's spinning around me now and I can't keep up. My head's pounding, and I was feeling groggy to start with, but with the added adrenaline it's awful.

"What's happened?" I look at Jana. "Start at the beginning."

"Phia worked today—she said she wouldn't. Mr. Richards touched her inappropriately before, and—"

"I saw him," Damien says suddenly.

"What? When?"

"Last week, when I was walking one of the dogs. I was in the woods—that walk that Marnie last took, it was the *same* route. And Mr. Richards was there too, walking that way with his dog."

Jana turns—a stormy whirlwind as her hair flies out—to Trevor. He's still got a phone to his ear. I think it's Jana's. "Are you speaking to that detective?"

He shakes his head. "Just on hold. They're connecting me to someone," he says. "But we can't just wait here. It's his house. Has to be his house. We can't wait for the police to show up. We have to go now."

"Hold on," Damien asks. "If he's abducted two women, this guy's going to be dangerous. We should wait for the police."

Abducted. My mouth dries. This is a crime. An actual crime. I look at Damien, feel breathless, but he's not looking at me. He's just shaking his head, looking worried.

"We don't wait when our friends' lives are in danger," Jana says.

Trevor's already out the door.

It's all happening so quickly, and I can't concentrate. Can't...can't process it.

The engine of Jana's car makes a slightly high-pitched whirring that seems to set my spine on edge. We're all bundled in. Jana's driving, Trevor's in the passenger seat up front, directing Jana, and Damien and I are in the back. I clutch my prescription like it's a lifeline.

I can't remember the last time I was in Jana's car. Not with my OCD…but I am now, and my head's spinning. And it's like time is wrapping around my body, squeezing tightly. One moment I'm taking a breath outside *The Red Panda* and the next we're hurtling through a housing estate.

"Slow down," Trevor tells Jana. "I think we've gone past number thirty-one."

Jana slams on the brakes, and the tires shriek. I'm thrown forward, and the seatbelt grabs me round the neck. A startled sound escapes my mouth.

Damien grabs my arm. "You okay?" His eyes are wide.

But I can't answer because Jana's shouting for everyone to look out the window.

"I already said!" Trevor yells. "That was thirty-one, with the red door."

My breaths hurtle through my lungs, and Damien's still touching my arm—but his fingers don't feel bad. Just cold. Ice cold. Or maybe it's me who's cold.

Jana reverses the vehicle at alarming speed before slamming on the brakes again, throwing us all forward. Damien sticks his arm out in front of me this time though, and I crash into his arm.

"That's it there!" Trevor says, and then he's opening his car door and jumping out. I've no idea where he got Mr. Richards's address from.

"Watch the traffic!" Damien shouts.

A car whizzes past us, but Trevor avoids it. Jana kills the engine, then she's out the car too.

"You okay?" Tenderness swirls in Damien's eyes.

I nod and stare at the flower air-freshener that hangs from Jana's rearview mirror. I place my prescription bag on the seat. "Let's go."

It's weird how when my heart's pounding and adrenaline's pumping through me that I almost feel like I'm not here. I sort of see everything as if I'm an onlooker, not part of it. See the four of us run up to the house. See how Jana pummels her fists on the door, how the door suddenly gives in—not very secure—and Jana falls forward. She crashes to her knees, and I know I'm standing right behind her, but my brain's doing funny things to the distance—I may as well be miles away.

Trevor and Damien pull Jana up, and then we're all inside and there's the strong smell of coffee and dog.

Dog. I look around nervously.

"Hello?" Jana yells, and she's shouting so loudly it feels like my eardrums might burst with the pressure of her voice. Because the air's too heavy too, squeezing around me, and Jana's still yelling. "Phia!"

"Marnie?" Trevor yells.

Damien turns to me. "Is this definitely the right house?"

I shrug. My head pounds. I can't make sense of anything. There's a loud thumping in my ears. it might be my heart rate. I can't quite tell.

"Marnie!" Trevor shouts. "Are you in here?"

"Oh my God, did you hear that?" Damien says, his voice low.

Hear what? Hear what?

But then they're all moving, and I'm numb as I follow. Nervous energy fizzles through my legs, and my heart rate's too high. My vision dims. Dark walls. Stairs. Going downward.

A musty smell. Thick, pungent. And something else—

Jana retches.

"Get that door open!" someone shouts, and my ears are distorting things, because I can't recognize it as Damien or Trevor. Or maybe it's me, I don't know. Everything's just too…

I need to get out of here.

I sink back into the shadows, but my arm catches on something. Something plastic. I flinch. It touched me. I'm contaminated, I'm—

Get out of here now! It's too dangerous. Too—

"Help!" a voice cries.

But I can't help. I can't do anything. My head's spinning.

THIRTY-EIGHT

Damien

"THAT'S PHIA!" JANA yells, her face red. She pounds on the basement door, rattles the handle, but it doesn't give at all. "Help me!"

I throw my weight at the door, and I can hear Phia on the other side.

"Phia? Is Marnie there too?" Trevor shouts. "Marnie? Are you there?"

Someone yells something, but I can't make out the words. I think it was Phia, though. She just sounds scared.

"Get back!" Trevor shouts from behind me. "Phia, move away from the door. I'm going to kick it down."

My heart pounds as I step away. Cara. Where is she? My eyes sweep the hallway for her, but I can't see her. Did she go back upstairs? Because she's not down here, not—

Trevor lets out a war cry as he kicks the door. There's a creaking sound, but nothing gives. I hear Phia crying on the other side.

"Try again," Jana hisses.

Trevor does, and then I try too.

"You need the key," Phia shouts. Her words sound a bit off though. Distorted.

"Here," Cara says, and she just seems to appear so suddenly. There's a key in her hand. I stare at her, shocked. She's holding it stretched out toward me, so the key's at arm's length. "It was on the kitchen table."

Jana snatches it from her, turns back to the door.

"Cara?" I move toward her.

She's staring at her hand, shaking. I've never seen her face so pale. Her fingers curl a little. Her teeth chatter.

"It's okay," I say.

"Yes!" Jana yells, and then the door's open. "Phia!"

Phia tumbles forward, falls into Jana's arms, red hair flying everywhere. She's gulping and crying and I see she's got a black eye. Her pupils look too large.

"She's back there," Phia whispers. "She…she might still be drugged… He drugged me at the café, and…"

"Marnie?" Trevor flexes his fingers for a split second, then he's running. "Marnie!" he shouts.

My chest rises and falls too quickly. I peer into the basement—can only see darkness.

"It's okay," Jana's saying to Phia. Cara's just behind them now, still shaking, still staring at her hands.

I move toward her. "It's okay." I try to keep my voice low, calm, but it breaks, gives away how scared I am.

Cara's gaze shoots to mine. She just shakes her head. Her eyes fill with tears, and then she's crying and—

"Marnie! Marnie, can you hear me?" Fear wracks through Trevor's voice. "Someone, help me!"

I jolt like I've had an electric shock, then I'm moving into the basement. Darkness and—

I nearly throw up as the smell hits me: it's what death smells like.

No.

My heart squeezes.

"Where are you?" I try to peer through the darkness.

"Over here." Trevor's voice is muffled.

Suddenly, light flicks on. Bright light that stings and burns. I blink several times, see Jana in the doorway, her hand on the wall. On a light switch?

Cara steps into the room, her movements uncertain. Her whole body tremors. Phia's right next to her. Cara moves toward me, but her eyes are strange, almost empty. Like she's not there.

"Cara! Get Phia out of here," Jana says.

I turn back, see Trevor kneeling over a slumped figure. His sister. He's mumbling something over and over.

Phia hurries toward Cara—and too late I realize what she's about to do: touch Cara.

And I watch in slow motion as Phia grabs Cara's arm. I see the horror in Cara's face, how her eyes glass over as she starts shaking.

"Just get her out of here and into the car!" Jana shouts, throwing her keys at Cara. They land short, clatter onto the tiled floor.

"It's okay," I shout to Cara. "I'll take her. I'll—"

"What the hell are you doing in my house?"

We all turn at the sound of Mr. Richards's voice.

THIRTY-NINE

Cara

SHE'S TOUCHING ME. She's touching me. She's touching me.

My head is spinning, and I feel sick and I can't focus on anything, not even on Jana's boss as he's shouting at us. All I can process is that Phia's clinging to me. Her fingers are like vices.

Mr. Richards storms forward. He's going for Damien and Trevor, where they're crouching next to something. No, someone. Marnie. It's Marnie!

"I've got a gun!" Mr. Richards shouts. "And this is my house and you're trespassing! Damn it, Buster, where are you?"

A gun.

My throat feels too tight. I can't breathe, I can't—

"Buster, get here now! Attack! Attack!"

I look up and see a dog. A Dalmatian. I nearly scream.

Trevor shouts and shouts and shouts, and then there's a lot of shouting. So much shouting. Just shouting and shouting and shouting. Jana and Trevor and Damien. And Mr. Richards.

And me. And the Dalmatian that isn't attacking. He's just standing behind Mr. Richards.

And the gun… Mr. Richards has a gun. Pain dives down my spine.

"Buster, Buster!" Mr. Richards is yelling. "Get them!"

I'm shouting. I realize it with a jolt, but I'm not shouting words. I'm just screaming. My head's pounding, and Phia's fingers are burning me. She's still holding onto me, but my OCD's quiet now. It's too scared. I'm too scared. I can't process anything.

Got to get out.

I try to move, try to drag my heavy legs, but Phia's anchoring me to the basement, and I can't get out. And Mr. Richards suddenly looms too close and—

I scream, and he's coming toward me. So close. I duck under his arm, pulling Phia with me, and the gun—he's waving it round widely. A jarring sensation fills one side of my face, and none of this feels real. My brain can't cope.

Someone punches Mr. Richards, and he staggers back, and I turn, see Trevor breathing hard, holding his fist. My heart pounds, and—

Sirens—I can hear sirens. I concentrate on them because I can't concentrate on this. This is too much. But the police are coming. Sirens mean they're coming. Sirens mean safety, right?

And it's not safe here. Trevor and Mr. Richards are fighting, kicking and punching and—

"Lock him in here!" Trevor shouts.

I have to get away. My heart pounds, and all I can think of is how I'm going to get away. Survival mode, that's what it has to be. Is that why nothing feels real? Why the moments are all merging together? It's just glimpses and flashes of moments, but I can't work out how much time has passed.

I turn. I'm free—Phia's not holding onto me now.

The keys. Jana's car keys. They're on the floor. My heart pounds. If I get them, I can get go to the car, I can lock myself in. Me and Phia. Where we'll be safe.

Safe. But what about Damien? And Jana? And Trevor?

My heart flutters. I can't leave them, I can't—

"Get Phia out of here!" Jana bellows at me.

I feel her words like they slap into my face. My skin burns at their touch, and then Phia's pulling at me again.

The keys.

I stoop and grab the car keys, and there's movement, so much movement in the basement. Arms and legs—and grunts, shouts.

Damien.

My heart twists. I can't process it, can't work out what's happening, can't—

"This way," Phia cries, and then it's like my body's unlocked, and I'm free to move, and we're running. Running up the basement stairs and through Mr. Richards' house, to the front door, where sunlight's spilling in.

A policewoman appears in the doorway so suddenly, like in a cartoon or something. She's shouting in her radio, and then she sees me and Phia. And Phia's shouting at her, and then Jana's behind us too.

Jana shouts more things, and my head pounds. Too many things are happening, and then…then we're outside.

"They'll be out soon," Jana says.

Damien.

My heart squeezes tighter and tighter, a python around it.

I watch the door, waiting for him. My breathing gets faster. Faster and faster, and minutes are clawing by.

Where is he?

"Damien," I whisper.

I wait and wait and wait.

More police go in. More shouting. And the first woman's trying to talk to me and Jana and Phia. Asking us what's going on. I hear Marnie's name mentioned, but I can't concentrate, I can't speak. My vision's swirling, and everything looks too small, too dark. My eyeballs feel gritty.

I wobble.

Jana grabs my arm. "Come on, sit down," she says.

And then we're sitting on the pavement. The dirty pavement. But I'm already contaminated… Can't get worse. My head pounds.

I look up and—

"Damien!"

He's out of the house. He's here, safe. And he sweeps toward me, drops onto the pavement next to me.

"It's okay," Damien says. "You're safe. We're safe."

I hug him. I just do it—it's instinct.

FORTY

"I WAS USELESS," I say, staring at my forefinger with the pulse-oximeter on. "Absolutely useless."

I wish the bed would swallow me up as more and more shame fills me.

I'm in hospital—and how ridiculous is that? I didn't get hurt. But the police insisted I got checked out. They said I seemed woozy, asked Jana if I'd banged my head. And she'd been trying to explain about the brain inflammation, and then as soon as they'd heard that, they'd bundled me straight in the ambulance with Marnie and Phia.

How embarrassing is that? I'm not even hurt, yet I'm here.

"You were great," Damien says. He's sitting at my bedside, having just spoken to my mum on the phone, reassuring her that I'm all right. Because I guess it would've been quite a shock getting a phone call from the police like that.

"But I wasn't great, not at all. I froze completely. I couldn't do anything." I feel sick just thinking about it. How utterly useless I was. How utterly useless I am at everything—because of the Lyme? Or maybe that's just me. Because some people freeze up in situations like that anyway. Maybe I'd have reacted the same if I wasn't ill.

"You got Phia out," he says. "And you didn't freak out when she grabbed your arm. Or when you brushed against the doorway. Or when we were sitting on the pavement. You did so well."

I can't help but feel like he's just saying those things.

A lone tear runs down my face—then I feel another and another. Oh, God, I'm going to ugly-cry in front of him. I gulp quickly.

"It's okay," he says. "It is—we're all okay. We found Marnie and Phia. I mean, how amazing is this going to be for the podcast?"

I let out a laugh. "We're still doing that?"

"How can we not?" he says, running a hand through his hair. "This is just too good an opportunity to miss. Four people in their twenties solve a crime the police say didn't exist *and* save a missing woman? Everyone's going to want to know our story."

Our story.

I like the way that sounds, and I realize suddenly that this is going to be something that cements us together. Not just me and Damien, but Trevor and Jana too. And Marnie and Phia. The six of us share this now.

I think of Marnie, the glimpses of her I saw in the ambulance when I wasn't panicking. She came around, was mumbling something incoherent at some point. I asked what was wrong with her, but the paramedics hadn't replied. They might not have even heard me. I suppose I was on the sidelines, in the back of the van on the fold-up chairs with Phia squeezing my hand and shaking. But I saw the bruises on Marnie's neck. Bruises that looked like strangle-marks.

Phia had a black eye, but I only really became aware of it in the ambulance. I asked her if she was all right, and she'd just nodded. Said Mr. Richards hadn't done anything to her yet.

Yet. That one word had made me feel even sicker as I looked over at Marnie.

"And you'll get better soon," Damien says. "You'll be able to start treatment again. I saw you got more on the GoFundMe."

I did? I stare at him blankly. "But what if I don't actually get better? What if I'm just always like this?"

He leans back in his chair and his jacket rustles. "We'll face that if it comes to it," he says. "But, Cara, even if you don't, it's not going to change the amazing person that you are. I fell in love with you in Mallorca. And I've fallen even more in love with you just in the last week, here. It's you I love. Your illness doesn't stop that."

Love? He loves me? I stare at him. My throat feels too thick, and my tongue too big for my mouth. And I should say it back—is that what he's expecting? The moment where we both profess our love for each other.

"It's okay," he says with a smile. "I know I come on heavy." He offers me his hand, and I surprise myself by taking it so easily. "We'll go slow with this."

I nod, and my head's spinning, and I drink in his eyes—the only stable points in my mind. My breaths come in short, sharp bursts.

He leans closer, and I'm staring at him. At his lips, now. How close he is. And he smells of sandalwood. Suddenly, the whole room seems to smell of it, of him.

I lean in close to him, shaking.

Our lips brush, tenderly at first, but then with slightly more pressure.

And we're kissing. I'm kissing Damien Noelle! My heart pounds, and adrenaline thuds through me, and I'm getting too self-aware, too self-conscious as we kiss. And I'm crying still.

But it feels right.

Damien pulls back and smiles. That's all he needs to do because the smile says it all. It tells me everything I need to know, because it makes his eyes lighter. Makes his eyes into a portal into his soul, and looking at his smile and his eyes, I see his soul.

And I know that he's right—everything will be okay.

FORTY-ONE

Cara

Three Years Later

"WELCOME TO THIS very special episode of *The Accidental Detectives*. Today, on the third anniversary of our very first episode, we'll be looking back at the case that started us off. The Marnie Wathem Case." Damien's voice is rich and authoritative as he speaks into the microphone, and just hearing him speak almost makes me fall in love all over again. "And, in a first for our podcast, we will be broadcasting this whole episode live, so this is a great opportunity to ask your own questions. Just tweet those questions to us, and we'll be answering a few across this episode. And of course, where would we be if we didn't have some amazing guests lined up?"

He nods at me.

I lean forward in my chair, still unbelieving that we have a proper recording studio now. And it's posh—so posh. Half the switches in here I don't even know what they're for. Plus, there's proper soundproofing and everything. And big fancy headsets for us all to wear. And the fact that I'm wearing the headset—having it touching my hair—still amazes me. Amazes me that it doesn't bother me. That the brain inflammation is getting better, even if it's a slow process.

"Yes. We have some amazing guests." I smile widely—even though I know that viewers won't be able to see me. But it's a habit I've picked up, since Damien and I have been doing this sort of professionally. It's amazing how our little podcast actually took off. I suppose finding two missing women helps a lot with making your true crime podcasts popular. I nod toward the guests sitting in a row beside me. "So, you'll be hearing live from Marnie Wathem and Sophia Byeon, the two abduction victims of Ronald Richards. We've also got Trevor Wathem and Jana Hargreaves with us, and along with Damien and me, we'll be chatting about the moment the four of us rescued Marnie and Sophia. Plus, we're also joined today by Maria Smithdale, the criminal psychologist who carried out the initial assessment on Ronald Richards when he was first detained."

"What a great episode this promises to be, with just that line-up alone!" Damien says. "But we've also got recordings of the police interviews with Richards too, including the initial one where he denied any involvement in the abduction of Wathem and Byeon. We will be playing these recordings on air, and then we will have the first-ever interview with Marnie Wathem. How amazing is that?"

"Yes, it is amazing, Damien," I say, and I think it sounds silly using his name like this, so often, but it was in the podcast coaching lessons that Mum got for me. "And we're just so grateful to both Marnie and Phia for giving us this opportunity.

So, let's start at the beginning, shall we? Let's get started on this special episode about the Wathem/Byeon abductions."

Damien presses play on our 'jingle' clip. As it plays, I look down the line at my friends. Jana gives me a big thumbs-up. Trevor's looking nervous, as is Marnie. Phia lifts her head up and then pushes her hair—now purple—behind her ears with precise, confident movements. Maria, the criminal psychologist, folds her hands carefully in her lap.

"On the 12th September three years ago, Marnie Wathem was out walking several dogs in the woods behind the town," Damien says. "It was a walk she did not return home from, and her brother, Trevor, reported her missing. The dogs she'd been walking were found in the early hours of the next morning, but bizarrely, the general consensus of the town of Brackerwood was that Marnie had simply abandoned these dogs by choice and run away at that very moment. The police were…"

As Damien sums up the whole case, I feel strange—I always do whenever we talk about it. I mean, loads of journalists wanted to interview us about the rescue. I did one interview at the time, but my Lyme was flaring. I couldn't even remember most of it—it was all this numbing fog in my brain, and even now I can only remember snatches. Little glimpses. The sight of Jana's car keys on the tiled floor. The shapes of Trevor's and Damien's bodies as they hunched over unconscious Marnie. The flower air-freshener in Jana's car. My Boots prescription on the seat in the car.

After a few moments, I find myself looking out of the window. It's an internal window, and on the other side are Mum, Dad, and Esme, along with a few other people who want to watch live as our audience. Mum sees me looking and gives me a toothy grin. I smile back, the warmth really eradiating inside me as I remember how I hugged her this morning.

I've been getting better on the private treatment. There've been a lot of ups and downs, but after a couple courses of IV antibiotics, my OCD and brain inflammation reduced substantially. I'm still getting used to hugging my family, but it feels amazing.

"…and all this time, the police simply weren't interested," Damien continues. "Even when the second victim, Sophia Byeon, was missing, and it was Trevor Wathem again reporting it, the police put him on hold. With no officers being sent to assist us, it really was left to us—a former waitress, an operations management worker, and Cara and I, two avid true crime fans—to rescue both Sophia Byeon and Marnie Wathem from the evil hands of Ronald Richards."

I lean closer to my microphone. "Now, to start with, we've got quite a few questions for you, Marnie. I mean, we're so excited that you're giving up your time today, and so, so grateful. So far, you've been quite closed-off in talking to journalists, so we were ecstatic when you agreed to come on our podcast. And we'd love to know why you chose us?"

Marnie licks her lips and then clears her throat. "It's because you were there. And you believed I was missing from the start. My brother told me." She glances at Trevor. She's nervous, but she's trying to hide it. "Told me how you approached him and wanted to investigate. So, I'm happy to speak with you—I literally owe you my life, anyway." She laughs. "A lot of the other reporters though, they only wanted to look at my case once I'd been rescued. They believed the runaway theory. They didn't want to help when help was actually needed."

"And we are so glad that we were able to help you," I say. "Do you mind if I ask you about the start of it all? The abduction and how it happened?"

Marnie nods. "Of course. Uh, yeah. I was walking the dogs, and I just saw Mr. Richards there. In the woods. I used to work for him at the café he ran, and things hadn't ended well. It was only a temporary job, but we all quit when we heard him being racist. So yeah, we'd had this argument after that—him telling us we were stupid and what he said was nothing—but nothing came of it. So when I saw him in the woods, I didn't really think anything would happen."

"You didn't think he was dangerous?"

"No. I didn't. He stopped me, though, in the woods. I had all these dogs barking, and he was just acting strangely. He had his dog with him too. A Dalmatian. But it looked scared of him, and I commented on it. God, I wish I hadn't, because that's when he hit me. He punched me right here." She points at the side of her face.

"So, he hit the left side of your face?" I say, for the listeners' benefit.

"Yes. And I was screaming, and the dogs were going crazy—that's the sound I remember. Nothing else. And then…then I woke up in his basement."

"Which is where we found you," I say. "So, let's talk a bit about the actual rescue then. As you know, I'm not an investigator or anything. I mean, at the time I was quite unwell with Lyme disease and usually my excitement for the day revolved around just talking to friends. And suddenly I found myself in a rescue mission. Now, we were looking for Phia at that point who'd just gone missing, but the moment we found you there too, in that basement, was just incredible. So, what was the rescue moment like for you?"

"It's a tricky question to answer," Marnie says slowly. "Because I don't remember it. First thing I remember is being in the hospital, with all these needles and wires sticking out of me. But you've no idea how many times I dreamed of people just busting their way in like that, in the weeks before. I was just waiting for help. I just wanted to get away from him. He..." She swallows hard.

Marnie was abused by Mr. Richards, multiple times. Damien and I have promised her that she won't need to talk about that on the podcast though. I try to give her a reassuring look.

She nods and then clears her throat. "When I woke in the hospital, it seemed too good to be true."

"Too good to be true," Damien muses. "I mean, it is a remarkable story. Four amateurs rescuing two missing women. And taking down Ronald Richards too!"

I zone out a little as the session goes on, but Damien notices and whenever it's my turn to speak, he gives me a little nudge before he asks me the question. Enough time that I can shake myself back to alertness. Plus, it's not like the questions are a surprise. We've been planning this episode for months.

By the time we're closing up the session, my back's aching a lot. My vision's blurring more too. I'm due my next lot of meds. They're in my bag outside, with Mum. If I sit up straighter and look through the window, I can see it on the chair next to her.

"And, now, to finish, I have one very special question to ask," Damien says.

I frown—what's this? We haven't planned any more questions, have we? Or have I forgotten? I squirm a little.

Jana nudges Trevor, and he gives her a look I can't quite decipher.

Damien swivels in his chair to look at me. "So, as all our listeners most likely know, Cara and I are together. And I just want to share something about how amazing this woman is, because she is amazing. I know Cara's mentioned it before, but I'm not sure you all really understand the extent of it. So, Cara's got neurological Lyme disease, and she's been having treatment for it for several years in order to control and try and treat the brain inflammation that this causes."

I inhale sharply.

"Cara has this amazing soul," Damien continues. "She's a fighter. A true fighter. She's the most resilient person I know, and it amazes me that she does all this—including rescuing missing women—while being so unwell. She is just amazing, and every time I look at her, I feel so lucky, so privileged to have her as my girlfriend."

I feel heat rush to my face. Oh, God. Am I supposed to say something? This is embarrassing!

I turn to look up at my parents—only to find that they're right by the window now, no longer sitting down. Mum's face is so close to the glass. Dad's behind her, and Esme too.

They're all *watching*.

"Cara," Damien says, turning toward me. He produces a small box out of his pocket and then he gets down on one knee. "Will you marry me?"

My heart pounds—pounds so hard like it's going to leap out of my chest—and I nearly laugh. This can't be happening! This can't be real.

I look around. See the smiling faces of my friends and family.

Jana nudges me.

And I turn and look back at Damien, see the ring he's offering.

"Yes," I cry, smiling—and I'm actually crying, tears running down my face.

Note from the Author
Living with Chronic Lyme

Cara's story is an especially important one for me, as I too have chronic Lyme disease. My battle with Lyme began shortly after I was sixteen years old. My family had just moved to a farm, and we knew there were ticks about—we saw them all the time and were forever removing them from our ponies and cat. Across the next four or five years, I'd been bitten by several ticks and developed the characteristic bullseye rash at least four times. My memory is still a little hazy as to the exact number of times this happened. Each time it happened, my GP gave me a short course of Amoxicillin. According to the NICE guidelines that the NHS follows, that should be adequate treatment.

But it's not—and it wasn't.

I became chronically ill, despite having been "successfully cured" of Lyme, according to my GP. Like Cara, I also developed Postural Orthostatic Tachycardia Syndrome and Chronic Fatigue Syndrome. My heartrate was too high, and then my blood pressure was also too low. I was dizzy and fainting. And so, so achy. No matter how much I slept, I never awoke feeling refreshed. Some days I could hardly move. My digestive system slowed right down, and I was constantly nauseous. My health was then complicated further by the development of Mast Cell Activation Syndrome when I was nineteen. And I thought that was as bad as it could get.

But worse was to come.

At the age of twenty-three, I developed autoimmune encephalitis which caused severe OCD and psychosis, just like Cara. I was put into the mental health system and doctors treated me like I was a hypochondriac. For over a year, the NHS refused to treat me for this brain inflammation. It was a battle to get anyone to listen to me, much less believe me. I felt like my whole life had been ripped away from me. I could barely do anything. It really was soul-destroying.

Most patients who have chronic Lyme disease in the UK have to seek private treatment. I was fortunate enough to be able to do this, after my family and friends crowdfunded thousands of pounds to cover the fees. My first lot of private blood tests—sent off to Germany and the USA—were positive for chronic Lyme (a condition that the NHS and many other health organizations deny exists). My lab report from Germany showed clear evidence of cellular immune activity against Borrelia Burgdorferi/Afzelii/Garinii—the bacteria involved in Lyme—while my low CD57+ cell count confirmed active infection. Additionally, I was also given the Cunningham panel blood test, which looks for high levels of autoantibodies targeting the brain, specifically the basal ganglia. My Cunningham Panel came back positive, with the detection of Anti-Dopamine Receptor D1 antibodies and Anti-Tubulin antibodies being way above the normal limit. This same test also found I had a raised Ca/Calmodulin Protein Kinase II level, which my private doctor told me was indicative of an active process.

Getting those results was such a relief. I wasn't a hypochondriac. It confirmed I was right—I *did* have chronic Lyme, and that was the cause of all my symptoms, including the neuropsychiatric ones.

I am now twenty-five, and I am still in treatment for this—it is a long process, and it's doubtful whether I'll ever be totally free of the effects of Chronic Lyme disease. But being ill like this has made me determined to raise awareness where I can. Because the more people who know about chronic Lyme, the more likely it is that others won't have to suffer like I did. And the more we talk about it, the more I hope that, at some point, the NHS guidelines will change. We need Chronic Lyme Disease to be recognized. We need to shout about it, and never stop shouting.

Acknowledgments

Writing this book has been so challenging, especially given that Lyme disease and asexuality are both topics that are close to my heart, and I really wanted to get it right. So many people have helped me with this book, and, for that, I'm eternally grateful.

To Isvari Mohan Maranwe: thank you so much for your insightful edits and comments and for being a cheerleader on so many occasions.

To Mariana Rodrigues and Sarah Anderson, my wonderful critique partners: thank you so much for giving such helpful feedback on this book (including reading countless drafts) and answering all my messages so quickly, even when I was panicking about this book.

To my team of wonderful beta-readers and proofreaders: Saffron Long, Linda Izquierdo Ross, James Parson, Roeshell McNelis, Jennifer Hutson, and K. Shirley. Thank you so much for all the time and energy you've spent on this. You've all really helped me make this a much stronger book.

And, finally, to my mum and dad and my brother: thank you for being there for me. Thank you for doing everything you could to get me the treatment I needed. Just, thank you.

About the Author

Elin Annalise writes contemporary novels featuring asexual characters. She graduated from Exeter University in 2016, where she studied English literature and watched the baby rabbits play on the lawns when she should've been taking notes on Milton and Homer. She's a big fan of koi carp, cats, and dreaming.

Elin's books include *In My Dreams*, *My Heart to Find,* and *It's Always Been You.*

CPSIA information can be obtained
at www.ICGtesting.com
Printed in the USA
LVHW050501140623
749708LV00003B/380

9 781912 369300